S0-ABB-755

Praise for Mackenzie McKade's
Merry Christmas, Paige

"Merry Christmas, Paige is a sexy, emotional tale of love, forgiveness and happiness... Ms. McKade has written a fast-paced story with memorable characters, plenty of heat and a touching plot that is sure to please readers and leave them with a smile on their face."

~ *Fallen Angel Reviews*

"Christmas is the time for miracles, including a second shot at happily ever after in this sizzling reunion story by Mackenzie McKade... Ms. McKade knows her way around, under, and through a love scene, and Merry Christmas, Paige definitely shows this. Readers are in for a naughty good time in Kauai as Nathan and Paige make up for five years apart, in every way."

~ *Joyfully Reviewed*

"Ms. McKade has done it again and has created a unique smoking-hot story full of love, loss, distress and danger... With this fast paced read, the reader won't even have a chance of thinking about putting the book down. If you enjoy reading contemporary romances where there are fantastic characters, smoking hot sex scenes and a fast paced plot with just enough danger to add a little extra spice to the story, this is a book you won't want to miss."

~ *The Romance Studio*

Look for these titles by
Mackenzie McKade

Now Available:

Six Feet Under
Fallon's Revenge
A Warrior's Witch
Lisa's Gift
Lost But Not Forgotten
Second Chance Christmas
Black Widow
Merry Christmas, Paige
A Little White Lie

Ties That Bind Series
Bound for the Holidays
Bound by the Past

Wild Oats Series
Take Me
Take Me Again

Print Anthologies

The Perfect Gift
Beginnings
Midsummer Night's Steam: Sins of Summer
Bound by Desire

Merry Christmas, Paige

Mackenzie McKade

A SAMHAIN PUBLISHING, LTD. publication.

Samhain Publishing, Ltd.
577 Mulberry Street, Suite 1520
Macon, GA 31201
www.samhainpublishing.com

Merry Christmas, Paige
Copyright © 2010 by Mackenzie McKade
Print ISBN: 978-1-60504-863-5
Digital ISBN: 978-1-60504-698-3

Editing by Sasha Knight
Cover by Scott Carpenter

This book is a work of fiction. The names, characters, places, and incidents are products of the writer's imagination or have been used fictitiously and are not to be construed as real. Any resemblance to persons, living or dead, actual events, locale or organizations is entirely coincidental.

All Rights Are Reserved. No part of this book may be used or reproduced in any manner whatsoever without written permission, except in the case of brief quotations embodied in critical articles and reviews.

First Samhain Publishing, Ltd. electronic publication: December 2009
First Samhain Publishing, Ltd. print publication: October 2010

Dedication

To my wonderful critique partner, Sharis Mayer, who makes sure I dot each "I" and cross every "T". To Kimber Osborne, Janet Reeves and Denise McClain for their expertise in the field of flight and medicine, and a special thank you to Ann Blackwood who introduced me to the beauty and legend of the naupaka flower. Thank you all!

Chapter One

Holding a sharp razor against a child's throat wasn't exactly how Dr. Paige Weston had expected to spend her Christmas holiday. Her hand trembled slightly. She fought to find her center through the worried cries of the boy's grandmother and the whispers of onlookers.

An airplane sucked as an operating room. So did the rudimentary instruments the flight attendant provided, but they would have to do. A calming breath helped steady her grip. She placed the blade against the child's delicate skin and began to press down. Without warning, the airplane bounced and dipped, knocking her sideways. She jerked her hand away. Her pulse raced. Nervous chatter filled the cabin as her stomach knotted.

"Dear God." She shot a desperate glance to the dark-haired flight attendant connected to Med-Link and the pilot. "Hold this airplane steady or—" The terror in Landon's grandmother's expression stopped Paige mid-sentence. The flight attendant who stood beside the woman didn't appear much better. She had turned as white as a sheet.

Slowly Paige exhaled and took a moment to gather her wits.

Time was ticking. Had it already been two minutes since Landon had fallen unconscious?

Steady or not, she couldn't wait any longer.

A thin line of blood swelled as she cut from left to right to expose the underlying membrane. A gasp rose from behind Paige, followed by a sickening thud as someone hit the floor hard.

Shit. Could anything else go wrong?

Paige blocked out the sound of hastened footsteps. A metallic scent touched her nose as she eased the razor deeper through membrane. Without being told, Joe, the flight attendant assisting her, dabbed at the blood with a gauze pad.

She pried the half-inch incision wide with two gloved fingers. "Tube."

Concern tugged at Joe's brows as he handed her the small piece of tube from the oropharyngeal kit. "Will he be okay?"

Paige didn't respond because she didn't know. The toy lodged in Landon's esophagus would have to be surgically removed. There was nothing she could do without a hospital, if she could even get the child to breathe again.

Easing the tube into the tracheal opening, she jabbed her free hand toward the flight attendant. "Tape."

Joe responded efficiently. As soon as she secured one piece of tape he had another waiting. When she was sure the tube wouldn't move, she grabbed the stethoscope hanging around her neck and pressed the end to the boy's bare chest to listen.

Breathe, she silently prayed.

Seconds passed and nothing. She had never lost a patient, and this was a hell of a time to start.

Was that a low whistle? She tensed, listening.

The first gush of air the child inhaled was followed by one of her own. The soft breath of life brought tears to her eyes and sent chills across her arms and legs. It was the sweetest sound she had ever heard. She attempted to blink away the emotion and focus on her patient's heartbeat, but her vision blurred momentarily.

Thump-thump. A strong, steady rhythm echoed in her ears. The boy's eyelids fluttered open, and she swallowed her gasp of happiness.

A smile slid across her face. "Hey, little man."

Several sighs of relief and even cheering rose from the onlookers, showing their support that Landon lived. When he became aware of the discomfort and the fact he couldn't speak, his eyes widened with panic. He attempted to jerk into a sitting position, but Paige eased him back down.

"You need to hold still, honey." Gently, she stroked his unruly brown hair. "Try not to speak. I know it hurts, but I promise you'll be fine in no time." Her voice seemed to calm him, so she began to sing like her own mother had done when Paige was a child. "Hush, little baby, don't you cry..."

The captain's voice came over the speaker, but she remained focused on her patient. She continued to soothe the boy, when Joe leaned closer. "We need to prepare the cabin for landing, but I'll stay with you if you need my assistance."

She stopped singing, but not the glide of her fingers through the child's hair. "I think we'll be fine." And for once she was right.

Landon remained quiet as the airplane began a diagonal approach. It was amazing how quickly the jet descended from the sky. No one seemed to notice the steep decline until the landing gears grinded like fingernails down a chalkboard. Within minutes the jet's tires touched ground. The jarring force threw Paige forward. She braced her palms on the floor to keep from falling, barely succeeding as the airplane rolled down the runway. Several mild jerks ensued before the aircraft finally came to a complete stop.

All at once the flight attendants began to move. In seconds the hatch was opened and emergency personnel entered with a stretcher.

"Dr. Weston," a young EMT said, kneeling beside her. "Would you like me to take over?"

"Yes. Thank you." She tugged off a glove, turning the latex inside out. Her job was done here. As she pushed to her feet, a sharp pang radiated heat across her lower back. The burning sensation was almost forgotten when the gurney passed by her, and Landon reached out and clutched her hand. Uncertainty and fear tightened his features. She attempted to ease her hand out of his, but he wouldn't release her.

Dammit. She had no resistance when it came to children. Their innocence, the way they trusted and accepted so freely, had always moved her. That's why she had chosen to become a pediatrician.

The EMT must have understood the struggle she fought, because he said, "You know it isn't protocol for you to accompany us."

The child squeezed Paige's hand again and her heart melted. Who could say no to a face like that?

After she ensured he was out of the woods she could take the next airplane to Fiji, where she had planned to celebrate Christmas with her mother and younger sister, Susan. Truth was, Paige felt responsible for the child. Leaving him without knowing the outcome would have been difficult anyway.

"Dr. Weston, if you're going with us we need to leave now," the EMT said.

She patted Landon's hand with her other one. "It's okay. I'll go with you, but you have to let me go so we can fit through the door." A tear slid from his eye. Reluctantly, he released her.

As she stepped upon the stairs leading to the tarmac, a

brisk wind tossed her long blonde hair around her shoulders. The sweet scent of flowers rose against the orange and red sunset that fanned across a graying sky. Déjà vu struck so hard she nearly missed the last step. She swayed, grappling to find her footing. Before she could shake the feeling, one of the EMTs called her name. "The hospital recommends you ride in back with us and Mrs. Buchman up front with the driver."

Paige climbed in the back of the ambulance and took a seat on the bench. Immediately the child grabbed her hand.

"I'm Scott," the EMT on the radio with the hospital offered. "This is Vic." The twenty-something man who adjusted Landon's IV line looked up and smiled just as the sirens blared and the vehicle jerked forward.

The airport was a blur as they rushed past it. Looking out the window, Paige ran one moist palm down her faded jeans and gave her T-shirt a tug. "I don't recall Honolulu's airport being so small when we touched down to pick up passengers. It looked larger."

"Pretty hectic on the plane, was it?" Vic's question drew her attention away from the window.

"Yes." An emergency tracheotomy on an airplane was a first for her.

Mischief twinkled in his eyes.

"What?" she asked. She could use a good laugh about now.

"You don't know where you are?"

"Of course, Honolulu." It only made sense that they would return from where they had previously landed.

"Nope. Welcome to Kauai."

Panic rose fast, icing her veins. Every bone in her body froze. She sucked in a tight breath. Maybe she hadn't heard him correctly. "Kauai?"

He pressed a stethoscope to Landon's chest. "Yep."

"Oh God. I thought we were heading back to Honolulu." She briefly closed her eyes and fought the sudden queasiness. This couldn't be happening. Kauai was one place she had sworn never to return to.

"There's been a cruise ship accident. The hospitals on all the islands are packed, including ours," Scott offered.

Her stomach pitched.

"Dr. Weston, are you okay?" he asked. "You look like you've seen a ghost."

She opened her eyes, but the memory of a sandy beach and the man who had broken her heart remained. The lump in her throat grew larger, but she managed a weak, "I'm fine." But she wasn't. Her whole body was one twisted knot.

It took her a moment to pull herself together. Besides, what were the odds that she'd run into Nathan on this island again? Sure, his parents owned an island just east of Kauai called Lotus Point. Even if he was in the vicinity, he would be on their family island—him, his wife and the child that should have been his and Paige's.

The thought struck like a dagger ripping through her chest. She flinched as the old wound tore wide open to steal her breath. How could it be that it felt like just yesterday Nathan had walked out on her, instead of five years?

A light squeeze of her hand pulled her out of the memory that threatened to consume her. She gazed down at the small hand holding hers, and then into the innocent eyes filled with concern.

You're being ridiculous, she silently chastised herself.

Ridiculous or not, Kauai was the last place she wanted to be.

When she had her emotions intact she forced a smile for the child. "What a good boy." She brushed damp hair from his forehead, and he relaxed beneath her touch.

Right now what she needed to do was focus on her patient. She would worry about getting the hell off this island later.

The trip to Wilcox Memorial took only five minutes, even with slowing down for red lights. On their approach, the siren was silenced. They pulled before the entrance where a team of medical personnel waited. When the ambulance stopped, the back doors of the vehicle swung wide. Immediately, Scott began to update a male nurse, while Vic worked with the others in attendance to unload Landon. The gurney wheels touched asphalt, and Paige and Landon's grandmother had to pick up the pace to keep up. The glass doors slid open, and she stepped inside to be assailed with cries and moans and the all-too-familiar antiseptic smell.

Lord, help them. The EMT had been right. The noise level bordered on offensive as medical personnel rushed in opposite directions. Thankfully, a surgical unit awaited Landon. Without delay, he was ushered through a pair of double doors.

Paige and Landon's grandmother didn't have to wait long before a nurse approached them. "Are you with the boy from the airplane?" The badge on her blue scrubs identified her as Cathy. By her dark skin and hair, she looked to be an islander.

"Yes. I'm Nancy Buchner, Landon's grandmother."

Cathy smiled. "Let me show you where the waiting room is. Admittance will be in to speak to you shortly."

When the nurse started down the hall, Nancy yelled, "Wait." She quickly moved toward Paige. "I can't thank you enough for all that you've done."

"You're welcome." Paige reached out and squeezed Nancy's arm. "He'll be fine. You'll see."

Nancy gave her a hug and then left with the nurse, while Paige remained behind. Paige looked around the busy ER room, locating a chair that was out of the way of the hustle and bustle. Next to the seat a colorfully lit Christmas tree blinked off and on. She sat down, and the light scent of evergreen tickling her nose reminded her that in less than a week it would be Christmas. Beneath the lower branches of the tree, neatly wrapped presents in cheery paper and big bows lay as if waiting for a cozy little family to open them.

A pang struck her chest. She swallowed hard, attempting to dash the image of a cozy family, mainly Nathan's, and focus on lying on the beaches of Fiji and soaking up the sun. Yep. Two wonderful weeks with her mother and sister. How pitiful did that make her sound?

Someone screamed in the room next to her and she startled. Her nerves crawled further out on the edge. What she'd give to speak to her mother.

Crap. Paige released a huff of disbelief. Her damn purse was still on the airplane along with all her luggage and cell phone. Nothing she could do about it this late at night.

This was going to be a long evening.

The minutes ticked by. Patients came and went. Several times Paige started to offer her assistance, but thought better of interfering.

A gray-haired man dressed in green scrubs and a surgical cap passed by the nurses' station heading straight for her. Slowly she got to her feet. Apprehension slithered up her spine. Dammit. Landon had to be okay. Her palms were clammy. She wiped them on her jeans just as the doctor stopped before her.

The doctor opened his hand, and in his palm he held a little red fire truck. "Here's your culprit. Wouldn't think something so small could cause such a fuss, would you?"

No, she sure wouldn't. Nor would she have guessed that when she got up this morning that her perfectly planned vacation would have taken the detour it had. Somewhere over the ocean an airplane was heading to Fiji and she wasn't on it.

"I'm Dr. Waters. Your patient is doing fine. He's in recovery. You saved that little boy's life."

Paige wasn't looking for praise. She worried more about the short time Landon had gone without oxygen. "A full recovery?"

"Yes. Thanks to you."

She exhaled a sigh of relief. "Good."

They shook hands, and Dr. Waters pivoted to leave, before stopping short. He glanced over a shoulder. "Don't imagine that you'd like to give us a hand in the emergency room? The cruise ship accident has left us in a bind. We're short a doctor and have one on vacation."

She didn't even pause. "Of course, it would be my pleasure, but I don't know when the next flight to Fiji might leave."

"I'll have someone check for you." He returned to place his palm on the small of her back and guide her toward the nurses' station. "I don't know if you are aware, but Wilcox Memorial is a leading medical facility and one of the top one hundred rural hospitals in the United States. Who knows, by the end of the night you might even want to join us. You know, we have an opening." He winked.

She chuckled. "Thanks, but no thanks. I'm just passing through." By tomorrow afternoon she would be back on track and far away from Kauai.

They stopped before the nurses' station, and a plump Polynesian woman with dark skin raised her head. "Ilana," Dr. Waters said. "This is Dr. Weston. She's offered to assist us tonight."

"Oh thank goodness." Ilana popped up from her seat and quickly moved around the desk to greet Paige with a hearty handshake. "Welcome. Welcome."

"Ilana will make sure you have everything you need, and she'll assign someone to contact the airport to check on the next flight to Fiji. Now if you'll excuse me," he said, "I need to prep for another surgery."

"Guess you might as well start at the top and work down. Let's see." The head nurse glanced at the dry-erase board. "Four-year-old girl with a laceration on the bottom of her right foot." She pulled a white jacket from beneath the desk and handed it along with the child's chart to Paige. She pointed down the hall. "Room five. A surgical tray has been set up. Teri will be in shortly to assist you."

No time like the present to get started. Paige slid her arms into the jacket, before starting off down the hall. Her sandals slapped against the cement flooring. She stopped at the door and knocked before entering. Peeking her head in, she said, "Hi. I'm Dr. Weston."

She couldn't help but notice how pretty her first patient was. Dark, shiny ringlets framed her petite face as big tears flowed down her cheeks. A young woman in her late teens or early twenties wrapped her arms around the child who sat on the examination table. Gently she rocked back and forth in an attempt to calm the girl.

"I want my daddy."

"Shhh, sweetheart. He'll be here in just a little bit."

Paige began to wash her hands. "So what do we have here?" She dried her hands on a paper towel.

"We were at the beach and Cami started to climb the rocks. They were wet from the rain, she slipped." The woman nervously brushed back her long brown hair. "It was an

18

accident."

"Of course it was." Paige stepped on the foot pedal of the trash can, the lid rose and she tossed the towel inside. When the door jerked open and struck the wall with its force, she startled. A man barreled through the doorway, his attention pinned on the child.

For a mere second the blood in Paige's veins froze. From the back he looked like— What was she thinking? It couldn't be Nathan, but that didn't stop her heart from pounding.

"Daddy," the little girl whimpered.

The man took the child in his arms and whispered, "Baby."

Oh God. The air in Paige's lungs escaped in one gush. She knew that deep, sensual voice.

"Janis, what happened?" Nathan asked.

As Janis explained the incident, the palpitations in Paige's chest began to pound with a vengeance. Her vision dimmed. She couldn't breathe. Just the sight of him made her knees weak. Rational thought escaped her as well. She had to get out of the room. She couldn't bear to see Nathan again.

Trembling, she moved quickly toward the door, stopping when the voice she'd dreamt about for five years said, "Paige?" Her entire body tensed. "Is that you?"

She clutched the doorframe like it was a lifeline. For one moment she felt she'd fall completely apart, and then she turned to meet her past eye to eye.

He smiled as if he was meeting an old friend. "Oh my God. I can't believe this."

"Daddy?" The tearful voice of the little girl forced Paige's attention from Nathan.

Cami was Nathan's daughter.

A sharp pain shot to Paige's chest. She swayed and the

room spun. She attempted to hold onto her professionalism, but it was like holding water in her hands. "I can't do this." She spun around and fled through the doorway.

Paige was halfway down the hall when a hand on her shoulder pulled her to a stop. Her arm flailed as she jerked away.

Ilana's eyes narrowed with concern. "Dr. Weston, are you okay?"

Paige pressed her hand to her mouth to restrain the cry being ripped from her diaphragm. The weight on her chest nearly suffocated her. If she didn't know better, she'd say it was a heart attack, but she knew this pain. It had become a part of her the day Nathan had walked out. Night after lonely night she had played the scene of his ex-girlfriend announcing she was pregnant a week before Paige and Nathan were to be wed.

Ilana waved Cathy over. When the nurse Paige had met earlier approached with a wheelchair, Ilana said, "Sit."

"Please." Paige's voice broke in short gasps as she bent at the waist, her palms on her thighs. She had to hold it together. "Give me a minute." She released the air from her lungs slowly in an attempt to steady herself, but the agony of seeing Nathan again threatened to pull her deeper into despair.

Ilana took the chair from Cathy and nudged it closer. "Why don't you have a seat while you catch your breath. You've been through a lot today. I'll let Dr. Waters know you're unable to continue—"

"No." The response came almost as fast as Paige snapping into a standing position. She wiped angrily at her tears. How humiliating. She had never dropped the ball on one of her patients.

You are a professional. You have a job to do.

She sucked in one breath and then another. She had to get

a grip. Like it or not, Cami Cross was her patient. After a few agonizing minutes, she squared her shoulders.

"Are you sure you're okay?" Doubt reflected in Ilana's concerned expression.

"Yes." Truthfully, Paige was anything but okay, but that was beside the point. She was a doctor. She could do this.

"Paige." Nathan's voice almost eradicated her brief moment of confidence.

She pinched the bridge of her nose and blinked hard, drying her tears. The beginning of a headache pushed at her temples.

"Paige?"

Heart in her throat, she turned to face her past. "Nathan."

Five years had a way of changing a person, but not him and not the electrifying effect he had over her. Her damn body went haywire, breasts tingling, as his gaze swept over them. The normal rhythm of her heart had yet to return, and now a heat wave flared across her skin. She couldn't take her sight off his handsome face. Broad forehead, lazy bedroom eyes and lips that were made for kissing taunted her. He had matured into an even better-looking man.

The urge to touch him was so great that she fisted her hands, gluing them to her side. Her nose tingled with the start of tears forming, but she had to stay strong. Somehow she had to get through this night without breaking down or losing the last bit of dignity she had.

Paige cleared her throat to steady her nerves. The sooner she finished up with Cami, the sooner Nathan would leave and be forever gone from her life, again. The thought was bittersweet, but she had no choice. He belonged to another.

"Paige, I'm so s—"

She silenced him with a raised hand. Without a word she hurried past him and headed for the examination room.

You can do this. She slipped through the open door and her feet pulled her to an abrupt stop. The sweet face of Nathan's child sent another wave of sorrow over her. Paige's daughter had his blue eyes and ebony hair. Her teeth clenched at the sting of tears. She swallowed hard.

Damn. Damn. Damn. She isn't your child and never will be. Let it go.

A single tear rolled down her cheek. To hide the emotion, she spun on her toes and headed to the sink. *You can do this.* She slid her hands beneath the warm water and scrubbed, maybe a little too long, but it was all she could do to refrain from running back out of the room. With a fragile grip on her control, she eased her foot off the pedal that activated the water before drying her hands. When she turned around, Nathan stood silently beside his daughter. His presence sucked the air from the room, making it difficult for Paige to breathe.

"My foot hurts," Cami whimpered.

"I know, baby," he said.

Paige closed the distance between them. Gently, she raised Cami's foot and examined the two-inch laceration. *Don't look at him. Focus on your patient.* It was difficult, but she did just that. The wound required stitches. "Did it bleed much?" Bleeding served as a natural way to cleanse the cut.

"Horribly," Janis said.

Janis was probably the child's nanny, because if she remembered correctly Nathan's wife was a haughty woman of wealth. Tall. Gorgeous.

Okay. That's enough. She mentally shook off the picture of the statuesque brunette. "Shots up-to-date, including tetanus?"

"Yes." Nathan moved to look at the injury.

She took a step backwards. His close proximity unsettled her in a way that made her want to flee again. What she'd like to do was bar him from the room, but that would be ridiculous and his daughter needed him. The logic didn't stop her from trembling. "Why don't we have the little princess lie down so I can get a better look?"

"Daddy, she called me a princess."

"She did, didn't she?" His deep voice raked over Paige's skin, making it prickle with goose bumps.

"Dr. Weston." Paige glanced over her shoulder to see a redheaded nurse enter. "Can I be of assistance?"

"Yes. Thank you. You must be Teri." Paige focused her attention back to Cami, but all she could see was the child that should have been hers and the man that would never be.

She pinched her eyes closed. *God give me the strength to make it through this night.* Then she raised her eyelids and went to work.

Chapter Two

Fuck. Nathan's hands were sweating, while Paige had an amazing calmness to hers. Nathan had always known she would be an outstanding doctor. She had a magical voice and touch. The way she spoke seemed to lull Cami into a sense of security and trust. Yet he knew what that voice was like when it turned dark and sexy, the heat in a mere whisper or the depth of emotion when she cried out in ecstasy. Her body arching against his as he—

Dammit. What was he thinking? He looked down at Cami and gave her a reassuring smile, but like a magnet his gaze was drawn back to Paige.

She hadn't changed, except for the maturity in her blue eyes and the sexy-as-hell way her curves and voluminous breasts filled out the T-shirt and jeans she wore. Light spilled over her beautiful features, including her full lips. He'd never forgotten how soft they were or the sweetness of their taste.

He still couldn't believe she was here—in Kauai—the place where he had met and fallen in love with her that summer five years ago. It must be fate.

Since his divorce would be final in a few days, he had purchased an airline ticket to Denver for the first week in January. He'd planned to surprise her.

Surprise her? Hell, what was he saying?

He hadn't called her before now because he was afraid she'd hang up on him. More than ocean lay between them. A phone call would make it too easy for her to dismiss him. He had to see her in person, beg her to forgive him, or at least listen to him.

Her reaction at seeing him again and the fact she avoided looking at him now only confirmed she hadn't forgiven him. And who could blame her? But why had she moved to Kauai? To torment him?

He willed her to meet his gaze, but she refused.

Did her hand tremble as she picked up the syringe?

Perspiration beaded his brow. He pushed his fingers through his hair. Truth was he had torn her world apart, but he had suffered too. Night after night, he'd dreamt that the woman lying beside him was Paige, not Sylvia. Sometimes he felt like a trapped animal needing to break through the invisible chains that held him.

Look at me, baby. Give me some sign that you still love me.

This time she raised her eyes and met his gaze head-on. Instead of the reassurance he sought, she held up the shot needle. He knew instinctively she had done so to alert him to the possible struggle they would have on their hands with Cami.

He leaned over his daughter as his palm moved to brace her right knee. "Do you remember when you fell off your bike and scraped your hand?"

"Uh-huh."

"Remember how the medicine burned for a moment and then you started to feel better?"

"Uh-huh."

"Dr. Weston needs to give you some medicine in order to

make you feel better. Okay?"

Cami tensed. She jerked her leg to no avail. "Daddy. No." Her chin began to tremble.

Damn. He hated that she had to go through this. "Ah, baby. Please."

Paige took a seat at the end of the examination table. "Cami, do you know the words to this song? Five little monkeys jumping on the bed." Did her voice shake?

The nurse joined in with a smile. "One fell off and bumped his head."

"Momma called the doctor," Cami whimpered, "and the doctor said." When the needle touched her wound, she jerked her leg, but he held her still. Big tears filled her eyes and spilled over her rosy cheeks.

"No more monkeys jumping on the bed," Paige finished up, patting Cami's leg and brushing his hand in the process. She quickly pulled away. "Uh. Or in this case no more monkeys climbing on the rocks." This time he was sure her voice quivered. She set one syringe down and chose another. When her gaze rose, it met his. For a moment she looked lost for words, and then she shook her head as if erasing him from her mind. "C-Cami, can you count to twenty real slow?"

Cami nodded. "One, two..."

"Slower." Paige cleansed the wound thoroughly, before retrieving the suturing needle. Deft fingers moved confidently. By the time Cami reached twenty, Paige had snipped the last stitch and set her equipment down. Without missing a beat, she stood and stepped around the examination table across from Nathan, but her attention was narrowed on Cami. "Gift wrapping your foot is the only thing left. Teri, can you please take over?"

The nurse smiled. "Of course."

Paige extended her hand to Cami and helped her into a sitting position. "Miss Cross, it was a pleasure meeting you." She paused. Her hesitancy and her edgy expression made him think she wanted to say more but couldn't or wouldn't. "Uh." She bit her bottom lip. "Merry Christmas." She released Cami's hand and pivoted sharply, heading toward the door.

He couldn't let her go. They had so much to talk about. "Paige."

Hand on the doorknob, she glanced over a shoulder. Her eyes glistened with unshed emotion. "She'll be fine. Keep the wound dry and clean. I'll order a prescription for antibiotics. Just follow the directions on her release papers. Goodbye, Nathan." She jerked open the door and rushed through it.

The finality in her goodbye sent Nathan into a tailspin. He needed to talk to her and dammit she would listen. Yes, this was all his fault, but he had suffered too. She had to know that he'd never stopped loving her.

As he headed toward the door, Cami whimpered, "Daddy?"

The desire to go to Paige was strong. It took everything he had to stop and turn around. "Yes, honey?"

"I want to go home."

"We will." He closed the distance between him and Cami. As he took her into his arms, he stared longingly at the door. "How long has Dr. Weston been employed here?"

Teri wrapped the pink elastic bandage around Cami's wound. "Oh, she isn't."

He raised a brow. "What?"

Teri quickly explained the events leading up to Nathan's surprise reunion with Paige. Another loop around his child's foot and Teri smoothed the edges of the tape down. "Since she was stranded, she offered to help out. What a godsend. I believe she's leaving tomorrow morning."

No. The silent demand echoed in his head. That meant he had less than twenty-four hours to apologize and ask for a second chance. "Where is she staying?" His question came out desperate, if Teri and Janis's startled expressions were a gauge.

"Uh. No plans that I'm aware of, but we are a hospital, beds we have." She yanked the glove off one hand, before dragging the other down. "I'll see if Cami's release papers are ready." She disposed of her gloves and left the room.

In five minutes Teri was back with the release papers and a wheelchair. Surprised by the speed of Cami's release, he couldn't help wondering if Paige wanted him gone as quickly as possible.

Hell. It didn't take a brain surgeon to see she didn't want to speak to him, but that was unacceptable. If there were no other choice, he would follow her to Fiji and let her know how miserable he had been these five years without her.

"As Dr. Weston said, keep the wound clean and dry. Here's the prescription. You should visit your family doctor in about ten to fourteen days to remove the stitches. Now how about a ride?"

He took the papers from Teri. "Janis, can you take Cami home? I'll get the prescription filled and be there soon."

"Daddy?"

"Maybe we can stop for ice cream on the way." Janis dangled the offer like a carrot.

Cami perked up. "Yay. Ice cream."

He raised her from the examination table, kissed her softly on the forehead and placed her in the wheelchair. "You girls be good." He watched as they disappeared through the doorway.

What if Paige had someone special waiting for her in Fiji?

The thought pulled him up short, made him dizzy with jealousy. Heat singed his ears. Would he stand a chance to win her back? Emotion tightened his chest and burned his eyes. So close to the only woman he had ever loved, and yet an invisible wall stood between them. Stepping out into the hallway, he saw Paige standing at the nurses' station. She glanced up and then away. As she hurried down the aisle, he caught up with her.

He placed a hand on her arm to draw her to a stop. "Can we talk?"

She swallowed hard, licking her lips like she always did when she was nervous. "There's nothing to say."

"I've missed you," he blurted.

He wasn't expecting a burst of laughter, but that's just what he got. "Yeah. I'm sure you have." Nor did he expect her sarcastic tone, which was uncharacteristic of her.

"Things have changed. I need to talk to you."

"Changed or not, Nathan, we're not the same people we were five years ago." She jerked her arm, but he held on tight. "Please let me go. I have work to do. There are people who need me."

She didn't slap him, but he felt the verbal blow and released her. Without another word she walked away.

Was he too late to mend the damage between them?

He sucked in a weighted breath. No. He wouldn't give up. This was just the beginning.

As she disappeared into a room, an old friend of Nathan's walked briskly past the nurses' station. "Hey, Jerry." He waved Dr. Waters down. "May I speak to you?"

"Nathan." The doctor shook his hand. "It's good to see you. Don't tell me your little one is here again."

Nathan shrugged. "Cut. Stitches."

The elderly man who played golf with Nathan and his father from time to time shook his head. "Kids. You got to love them."

"Tell me about it." Nathan cleared his throat. "Can I speak to you about Dr. Weston?"

A frown pulled at the corner of Jerry's mouth. "Everything okay?"

"Yes. I was just wondering if you could do me a favor."

"Sure. What's up?"

A second chance, Nathan prayed, as he shared his plan with his old friend.

One a.m. and Paige's feet and back ached. She collapsed into a big comfy chair in the physician's lounge. The fresh scent of flowers caressed her nose. The *rat-a-tat-tat* of rain pelting the windows announced the weather had intensified. Her eyes felt leaden, her heart even heavier. A chill swept across her bare arms. She rubbed her palms up and down her goose-bump-covered flesh, not finding the warmth she craved.

Between patients she had called the airport about her purse only to discover that all flights flying in or out of Fiji were cancelled due to unexpected weather, including the one Ilana had booked her on today. Threat of a hurricane near Fiji had everyone unsettled. According to the airlines, even Kauai and all the nearby islands were experiencing the fringes of the rain and wind. The authorities had suggested locking things down tight as a precautionary measure.

She'd thought hurricane season was over.

"Paige, your luck just keeps getting better," she muttered, closing her eyes. What the hell was she going to do now? What about her mother and sister? Talk about a screwed-up vacation.

"Tired?"

She pried her eyelids open to see Dr. Waters standing over her. So exhausted, she hadn't even heard him come in. "A little," she admitted.

"There's a taxi outside of the emergency lobby to take you to your hotel, courtesy of the hospital."

"You didn't have to do that. I can sleep in this chair." It's not like she hadn't done it before.

"Uh-uh." He offered his hand and helped her to her feet. "Not on your life. If there is even a minimal chance you might stay with us, I'll make sure you're treated right. Besides, we islanders pride ourselves on our hospitality."

"I appreciate it, but it really isn't necessary." All she needed was a couple hours of sleep, and then it would be late enough to call her mother and sister. Maybe she'd catch a plane back home, spend Christmas by herself.

"Yes. It is. Now get out of here. Perhaps you'll come visit us in the morning." He grinned ear to ear. Instead of shaking her hand he gave her a big old bear hug.

How could she not accept his gift? Besides being emotionally drained, she could use the solitude to lick her wounds. "Thank you. Oh crap."

"What?"

"My luggage. I don't have anything to wear." No toothbrush, toothpaste, deodorant, clean underwear, pajamas, nothing.

He glanced toward the table where a bulging plastic bag sat. "That's been taken care of. Teri raided our supplies and the gift shop. Remember, around here you don't need much more than a bathing suit and suntan lotion."

"And an umbrella, judging from outside."

He chuckled. "It usually doesn't last long. Now, get out of here."

Paige had to admit a soft mattress would feel better than a chair or the stiff beds that a hospital offered.

She thanked him and took the bag. On her way out she saw Ilana. "How's Landon doing?"

The woman looked up from her paperwork. "Sleeping. They moved him to his room."

Paige smiled with relief. Even the tension strung tight across her shoulders seemed to ease.

They exchanged good nights and Paige made her way toward the exit. The minute the glass doors swung wide the scent of rain hit her. There wasn't a star in the dark sky, only heavy clouds. The rain had lessened to a drizzle.

A roly-poly man in a floral shirt jumped out of the taxi in the driveway. "Aloha, Dr. Weston." A big grin greeted her. "My name is Feleti. Welcome to Kauai." As he approached, he slid open the umbrella in his hand and held it over her.

"Aloha." She dashed to the car with Feleti in tow. He opened the door and she ducked inside, placing the bag on the seat beside her. Quickly, he moved around the car and sat behind the wheel. Engine running, he shifted the car into gear and they were off.

Polynesian music played a lively tune on the radio. The steel drums and marimbas painted a seductive picture of the ocean, sand and swaying palm trees. Five years ago she had become drunk on the exotic music, Kauai and Nathan. Now, none of them held any excitement. She still couldn't believe he had insisted they speak. What was there to say?

"Vacationing?" the driver asked.

"Just passing through." She didn't elaborate.

"Unlikely." His deep laugh of disbelief held a rich tone. "Everyone falls in love with Kauai." He started to whistle to the music.

Who whistled at one thirty in the morning?

Headlights bounced off the wet road, the glow mesmerizing. Her last thought was *Where the heck is he taking me?* before she fell asleep.

"Dr. Weston." Through the cobwebs in her mind, Paige heard her name, but she refused to wake. She was so exhausted. Sleep. She needed sleep. A gentle shake forced one eyelid open. No more than a foot away from hers, the cheery, round face of Feleti invaded her space. "We have arrived." He stepped back.

"Arrived?" Disoriented, a queasy sensation rumbled in the pit of her stomach.

"Yes, ma'am."

She took a little time to gather her thoughts before climbing out of the vehicle. That's right. The hospital had rented her a room, but as she glanced around she couldn't believe her eyes. Instead of a touristy hotel, a secluded cottage stood before her. Light shined from its windows as if it was occupied. She took a step, hesitated before taking another. Her eyes rolled heavenward. This couldn't be happening.

"Fuck." She didn't usually drop the F-bomb, but staying here was not an option. This couldn't be coincidental. Yet there was no way Dr. Waters could have known she and Nathan had stayed here so many years ago. The vegetation was thicker, but she had no doubt as to where she was. The small cottage perched on a cliffside was the same place she and Nathan had fallen in love. A natural stone path led to the white sandy beach below. From where she stood she could hear the breaks crashing against the shore.

Then again, not everything was the same. Five years ago they'd carved a heart and their initials into a large koa tree that stood out front of the bungalow. The tree was gone now, just like their love.

"Is something wrong, Dr. Weston?"

Her stomach churned, twisting into knots. "There's been a mistake."

"No. The message I received specified this address." He dug in his pocket and retrieved a piece of paper with something scribbled upon it. "Yes. This is it. The key should be beneath the mat. Would you like me to carry your bag?"

"Bag?" She had nearly forgotten the only thing she had with her. Suddenly, a weighted breath pushed from her lungs. She truly had not a thing to her name. "I don't know how to say this, but it appears that everything I brought with me is in Fiji. That includes money. I can't pay you for the ride."

As he reached into the car and retrieved her bag, he chuckled. "No worries. The good doctor took care of that too."

Of course, the good doctor.

How ungrateful would she be to ask Dr. Waters for different arrangements?

There was nothing she could do but say, "Thank you," as she accepted her bag. No money. No credit cards. Her stomach growled. No food. Tomorrow she would spend the day locating someplace to wire her money. That is, if she could get someone to give her a ride into town.

This sucked. Tired and emotional, she didn't know how much more she could take.

"Would you like me to escort you to the door?" Feleti asked.

"No thank you." She knew the way, but couldn't quite get her feet to move. When he didn't immediately drive off, she realized he was waiting for her to go inside. So, with as much courage as she could muster, she walked to the door and bent down. Sure enough, there was a key beneath the mat. Her hands shook as she held the doorknob, inserted the key and twisted. Taking a deep breath, she pushed the door open and stepped inside.

Paige covered her mouth with a palm. Emotion rose to a crescendo that threatened to release the tears welling in her eyes. Everything was exactly how she remembered. The spacious living room designed in island décor with bamboo trim on the couch, chair, coffee table and matching wall unit that housed the television. Even the open kitchen hadn't changed, down to the single naupaka flower adorning the glass tabletop. White with purplish streaks, the petals formed only half a flower. Like a moth to a flame, she was drawn to the blossom. Her hand trembled as she picked it up and pressed it to her chest. She closed her eyes, unable to face what the flower represented. Loneliness.

As if it were only yesterday, she heard Nathan's sensual voice caress her ears as he told her the story. "The legend says the naupaka flower represents lovers who were tragically separated by the gods."

A tear rolled down her cheek with the thought of how their lives paralleled that of the legend. Fatefully divided—never to be together.

Why hadn't she stayed on that airplane? Why couldn't she forget and move forward?

Instead Nathan's words continued to haunt her. "One lover banished to the mountains, the other to the ocean's sandy beaches to live eternity alone."

The pain in her chest squeezed, the anguish almost too difficult to bear. Night after night, she went to bed alone, hoping that one day he would come and get her, but he never did.

"Please stop." The cry came out a whimper. Still holding the flower, she cupped her hands over her ears. She willed the thought of him to vanish, but his cruel words continued, slicing through her like a knife opening wound after wound.

"Only when we unite as lovers will the halves be whole again and joined forever."

Paige couldn't take any more. A river of tears burst beneath her closed eyelids. Her legs buckled and she dropped upon her knees. The desperate gulp of air she sucked in caught in her throat. Shudders raked her body. Her chest hurt so badly she felt like she was dying.

"Please, baby, don't cry."

She choked on a sob. The voice couldn't be real—he couldn't be real. It had to be just a vivid memory. Yet when she opened her eyes and looked over her shoulder Nathan stood in the doorway of the bedroom like he had that summer, the other half of their naupaka flower nestled in his hand.

She fought her tears, but they continued to race down her cheeks. God. This was humiliating. She didn't want him to see her like this.

He stepped beyond the door and approached. "Like this flower, we belong together."

Were those unshed tears in his eyes?

He knelt before her and plucked the other half of the flower from her hand. He pressed them together to form a perfect blossom. "See?"

"Why are you here?" Despair almost crippled her. Did he think this was a game? That her feelings could be played with and then tossed aside once again? Seeing him today didn't change anything. He was married.

God. She was tired. Her shoulders drooped.

"I had to talk to you," he said.

When he reached for her, she crawled away on her hands and knees like a wounded animal to get away from him. "Don't touch me," she snapped. She couldn't take losing him again. It would kill her.

Paige's tears raked at Nathan's heart, but her rejection stung even more. Slowly, he got to his feet. He didn't dare approach her. The strong exterior she wore at the hospital had crumbled the second she stepped foot into their cottage. Even the air felt brittle and volatile around them.

"Do you know how many times I have visited this cottage, stood on the balcony overlooking the ocean and wondered where you were? What you were doing? So many times I thought of finding you and bringing you back."

"But you didn't." Her words were followed by an eerie silence. He couldn't escape the helplessness in her eyes that only wavered when she spoke again. "Tell me, Nathan." Her tears seemed to dry instantly. She swayed getting to her feet. "What's your secret in letting go and going on with your life?" The bitterness in her tone was unmistakable. "How did you forget everything between us, walk away like we never loved before, because I didn't forget—couldn't." She clenched her teeth. One tear fell and then another one. "Every night I prayed for you to choose me, come for me, but you didn't." She paused. "I would have loved and cared for Cami like she was my daughter, but you never gave me the chance." She took a deep breath and held it, before releasing it in one long stream. Then she shrugged, almost as if she were dismissing him. "It doesn't matter anymore."

"Don't say that. It does matter." Nathan's throat swelled with emotion. He had to get her to understand. "I didn't forget us. Paige, you have to believe me."

Skepticism showed in the brow she cocked.

Dammit. This wasn't going as he'd planned. What a dumbfuck he was. Had he really expected her to welcome him with open arms? The thing that disgusted him the most was that Paige was right. Why hadn't he considered marrying her? He could have worked out a parenting schedule with Sylvia. Hell, that's what he had been doing the last two months in court.

God, what had he done?

Nathan had never felt so vulnerable, even scared. Clearly they were teetering on a thin line between love and hate. He loved her. She hated him. He kept his distance and chose to sit upon the couch, hoping the position was less intimidating. "Just hear me out. If you want me to leave afterwards, I will."

With angry swipes of her hands she wiped away the last of her tears and presented him with her back. She walked to the sliding glass doors and stared out into the darkness. What was she thinking?

He didn't have to wait long to find out.

"There's nothing to say." She paused before pivoting on the balls of her feet. "For God's sake, Nathan, you're married." The loathing in her tone was hard to miss.

He pushed to his feet and took one step toward her. "No, I'm not. I mean, I won't be soon."

Her eyes widened. "What?"

"My divorce will be final in two days." He ventured closer. "I couldn't continue living a lie. I didn't love Sylvia. You know I never did." He stepped near enough to touch Paige, but didn't. "There's only one woman I've ever loved. You." He set the intertwined naupaka flowers on the table. "Hell, baby, I have an airline ticket to Denver. I thought after the holidays, after the dust settled, I'd come see you and beg you back."

He watched for a crack in her resistance, but didn't detect one until she said, "I can't think clearly."

"Do you still love me?"

"Love?" He didn't miss the emptiness in the word or the chill in her blue eyes. "You loved me when you walked away, chose another woman. Do you have any idea what that did to me? What I've been through these last five years? I nearly died when you walked out on me. I can't go through that pain again."

Shame and regret pounded on Nathan as hard as any man's fist. "I don't know what else to say except I'm sorry. I made a mistake."

She pinned him with a steely glare. "I don't know if it hurts more that you don't know what to say or that it took you five years to come to that realization."

Lord, the woman was relentless and who could blame her. "Give me a chance to make it up to you. Please."

"I can't." Without another word she pulled the sliding glass doors wide and stepped into the darkness.

Sounds of the ocean and the scent of rain filled the room as he stared at her silhouette. She couldn't be lost to him.

If it was the last thing he did, he would find a way to break through her barrier. He would never stop pursuing her—never.

Chapter Three

Cross-legged, Paige sat on the bed, the telephone in her lap. "Mom, I don't know what to do." Her eyes were swollen, her voice nasally from crying. "All flights out of Kauai are cancelled. I'm stuck here." For how long, she had no idea. "I need to get off this island now."

"Calm down, honey."

"Calm down? Mom, that's not much help," Susan chimed in on the extension. "Paige, I say kick his ass." Her feisty younger sister would have an offhanded comment like that.

"Now that won't solve anything. Hang up the telephone, Susan," their mother said. "Sweetheart, you've been down this road before. You don't want to go down it again."

"Do you?" Her sister's tone softened.

That was the problem. Everything Paige had ever wanted was there for the taking, but what would the cost be? Nathan had betrayed her once. He chose another woman over her. Could she ever trust him?

"Maybe he's changed. Maybe this time everything will work out for the two of you."

"Susan, I can't believe you're saying that. One minute you want Paige to kick his butt, the next give him a chance."

"But, Mom, she loves him."

Her mother released a heavy sigh into the telephone. "I know."

Holding the receiver with one hand, Paige buried her face in her free palm, more confused now than before. "I'm tired." She hadn't slept a wink last night. The cottage haunted her with the ghosts of their time together. Every room held a memory, every memory a reminder of what she had lost. "I think I'll call the airlines again." She raised her head and looked around the room. She used to love it here, but now all she could think about was leaving.

"Sweetheart, I'm worried about you."

"Mom, I'll be okay. I need a nap, and then maybe I'll go to the hospital." At least she would be busy and closer to the airport just in case something opened up. Hell. She'd go to Timbuktu if she had to.

"Do you want me to wire you money?"

"No." She had made a telephone call to her bank. They were arranging everything through one of the banks here. During one of her night excursions through the cottage she had discovered the refrigerator had been stocked with food, but who could eat? Maybe it would be better if she just hid out in the cottage until the weather cleared.

A knock on the door made her heart skip a beat. She cupped the telephone. "Oh God," she whispered into the receiver. "I think he's here. What do I do?"

"Honey, what do you want to do?" her mother asked, while Susan remained unusually quiet.

From out of nowhere, a dam of tears burst. The sudden pain in her chest felt like her heart had been torn asunder. "I want—" Sorrow and grief rose so quickly it stole Paige's breath. "I want to quit hurting." Her anguish was so gut-wrenching it bled from the very depths of her soul. She couldn't speak. When she did, the mask of anger she'd used to cover the truth dissolved. "I want to run into his arms." She covered her mouth as if she could restrain the flood of emotion spilling out. "I want to forget these last five years." She sobbed uncontrollably. She pressed a hand to her chest, which heaved with each ragged inhale/exhale. "I-I don't want to be alone anymore. Mom," she choked, "I love him. I love him so much that it feels like I'm dying." Paige's confession was followed by an unladylike snort.

"Oh, Paige. Sweetheart. Please stop crying," her mother begged, as she wept right alongside Paige. Even Susan participated in their cry-fest, her sniffles coming over the telephone loud and clear. "Dammit. You should have never gotten off that airplane."

But she had and for whatever reason fate was taking another shot at her. A tremor raced through her. She struggled to rein in her emotion, to squelch the tears that refused to stop.

"Don't answer the door." Susan's voice quivered. "Pretend you're not there."

Like that would work. Paige had no transportation—no money. By now Nathan would know she was stranded. Besides, it was midmorning. Where else would she be?

Another knock, but this time it was harder, louder. "Paige, I know you're in there."

She stared out the window at the gray sky and the falling rain. The ocean churned with the same ferocity as the acid in her stomach. "It's him. He knows I'm here." Her tears slowed, but not the shudders raking her body. "I need to go."

"Will you be okay?" Concern raised her mother's voice.

No, but she said, "Yes."

"Will you call us?" Susan asked.

"When I can. Bye." Slowly Paige hung up the telephone and

set it aside. Her legs felt leaden as she uncurled them. Wiping at her remaining tears, she got out of bed, catching her reflection in the mirror. Dark circles, swollen eyes. She looked like hell, and there was nothing she could do to hide the fact she'd been crying.

Another knock made her tighten the sash around the soft cotton robe she wore. Ready or not, she had to face the music. Tell Nathan goodbye for the last time.

The floor was cool beneath her bare feet as she made her way through the bedroom into the living room. The naupaka flower lying on the table caught her eye and she paused to look at it. Amazingly, the two parts were still joined.

"Paige, open up. Please. I need to talk to you."

She briefly closed her eyes and prayed she could get through their encounter and remain whole in the process. It had taken her too many years just to accept that they would never be together. She pressed her hand to the door and knew this was the closest she could ever be to Nathan.

He knocked harder, the door shaking.

Her trembling fingers folded around the doorknob and she twisted.

The minute Nathan saw Paige's tearstained face, guilt rode him hard. For a moment he didn't know what to say. "Are you okay?"

The small chuckle she released held no humor. "What do you think?" She held the door only slightly ajar, as though trying to stop him from entering.

Without hesitation, he pushed the door wide, forcing her to step aside so he could enter. "That I've betrayed you and hurt you so badly you don't ever want to see me again."

"Then why are you here?" She sounded so lost. She pulled the robe around her like a shield.

"Because I love you." He resisted the urge to reach for her. "You may not believe me, but I dreamt of holding you every night. The last five years have been hell."

"Nathan, I don't want to hear this. You have no idea what hell is." She walked away from him to the sliding glass doors and gazed across the panorama. "What we had is over."

Please God, don't let her believe that.

He eased up behind her. He flexed his fingers before placing them on her arms. Carefully, he guided her around so that their eyes met. "No. It isn't. You know it and I know it." The anguish in her expression made it difficult for him to continue, but he did. "I've wronged you. But, baby, I never stopped loving you." Every nerve in his body sizzled like they were ready to ignite. He had to make her understand. "Paige, I was torn with the news that I was going to be a father. I should have held my ground. I should have married you." The tears in her eyes made his mist. "You're right. We could have had a life together and worked something out with Sylvia, but I didn't think." He looked away briefly, ashamed that he hadn't thought of all the options available. Why hadn't he seen a way out? "I've paid every day for the choice I made. Please don't make me continue to pay."

Pain like he had never witnessed hardened her features as she shook out of his hold. "You hurt me." Her voice cracked. "I don't know if I can ever trust you again."

The truth pierced his heart. The foundation of their relationship had been built on trust. Now it was gone. "Do you still love me?" he whispered.

"It's not that easy."

A sliver of hope burst through the gray clouds in his mind. She didn't say no. There was a chance, maybe a thin one, but a chance if he could get her to lower her guard. Then he would love her with every ounce of his being and show her she could trust him.

"It could be," he said softly. He retrieved the naupaka flower from the table. Returning, he caressed her hand with the blossom. "We can give the legend a happy ending. Take the flower, Paige. Tell me you love me and that you'll give me the opportunity to prove my love for you."

Licking her lips, she stared at the flower before turning away. "It doesn't matter if I love you."

"Then you do love me?"

She sniffled. Her fists clenched. "Don't do this to me, Nathan."

"Paige, all I want is for us to be together. Do you love me?" he repeated firmly.

She nibbled on her lower lip, silent tears racing down her cheeks. "I shouldn't. God knows I shouldn't, but I do."

Inside of Nathan a light of hope illuminated the darkness that he had lived with for five years. His chest tightened to the point it felt like he would burst. He tried to hide the joy that filled him, but it was useless. He opened his arms. "Come here, baby."

She stared at his arms as if he was inviting her into a trap. It stung to know he had pushed her to this extent, hurt her so badly she hadn't been able to go on with her life. He was a selfish bastard. She had remained his all these years, while he had attempted to make a life for Cami.

"Come here, baby," he repeated.

"I can't." Yet she took a step toward him.

"I'm so sorry. Give me the opportunity to make things right. Let me make up for the time I have stolen from us. Let me love you, Paige."

When the breath she held audibly released, her resistance melted too. She nearly flew into his arms, clinging to his neck like she would never let him go. She wept heart-wrenching sobs.

"Please, Paige." His voice trembled. "Don't cry." His eyes stung, his tears joining hers.

She felt so right in his arms, even better than he had remembered. He buried his face into her hair and inhaled the familiar scent of her perfume. Sultry jasmine and something fruity surrounded him like a blanket. "I've missed you so much," he admitted shamelessly. "Every night—every day."

The need to kiss her was overwhelming. He captured her lips with a hunger that scared him. His lips opened hers and his tongue plunged deep, searching and pushing against hers. She whimpered, the soft sound more of a cry than a moan. She tasted so fucking hot, a fire inside his soul that a mere caress could not extinguish.

"Love you," he murmured against her lips. Would he ever be able to convince her of the depth of his love? He kissed her frantically. A rough growl left his throat as his mouth slanted across hers again.

His unsteady steps drove her backward, pinning her against the cool glass door. Their bodies pressed together felt amazing.

She mewled, and he captured her mouth with another kiss.

The urge to strip her naked and take her now like he had dreamt of for so many nights was strong. Blood rushed to his groin, the heat shooting all the way to his head. His thoughts whirled. Over and over, he stabbed his tongue in and out of her mouth, while he mimicked the actions with his hips, seeking relief that didn't come. Instead he grew impossibly harder, his cock pressed angrily against his zipper. The only way to ease the ache would be to make love to her right here, right now.

She gasped, but her cry was muffled by his starving mouth. His lips moved over hers, his tongue skimming her soft palate. When she tugged at his T-shirt, a shiver raced up his back.

She jerked away, breaking their embrace. Her eyes were dark with desire. "I need you, Nathan. Make love to me."

Briefly, he closed his eyes and tried to hold on to what was left of his control. "I've waited a lifetime to hear you say that."

He took the flower from her hand and placed it on the glass table. When he returned he undid the sash of her robe. Skin like silk met his palms as he smoothed the garment off her shoulders. The air in his lungs caught at the sight of her. To his delight she wore nothing beneath the cover-up.

Firm breasts. Sensuous curves. She was perfection.

Dammit. His hands shook as he reached for her. She came willingly, even eagerly, into his embrace, which made him quiver with excitement. He trailed a path of kisses down her neck into the valley of her breasts. The feminine scent of her skin made him drunk with desire. His arousal intensified as small bumps formed on her areolas. Rapid breathing forced her voluminous breasts to rise and fall, again and again.

"You're beautiful." There wasn't much more to say, but he found himself continuing. "Do you have any idea how much I want you?" His fingertips danced across a nipple that grew taut. He squeezed it between his thumb and forefinger. She trembled in response and arched into his caress.

"Nathan. Please."

"What do you want, baby?"

"Shirt. Take it off."

Even if he had wanted to he couldn't refuse her. He needed

her as badly as she appeared to hunger for him. In one swift move he pulled his shirt over his head and tossed it aside to join her robe on the marble floor.

The second he leaned in and their chests touched it felt like fire surged through his veins. She was a living flame lighting the lonely corners of his life these past five years had darkened.

Caressing her neck with his mouth, teeth and tongue, he moved his hands down her back. "You feel so good." A raspy groan pushed from her lips as his hands glided lower to feel the soft mounds of her ass. "I've missed you so much."

"I need you inside me," she whispered in his ear. The seduction in her voice made his balls pull tight against his body. "Love me, Nathan." Desire burned like a candle in her smoky blue eyes. Her heated expression made his cock jerk.

His fingers intertwined with hers. Without a word, he led her toward the bedroom and the bed where they had made love so many times that summer. Rain sliced sideways, driving past the balcony cover to pound against the window. The small gate of the spiral staircase banged back and forth as the wind blew.

With a feather-light touch, he kissed her, before laying her back on the bed and following her down. "I can't believe you're here." When he lowered his head, their gazes locked and her breath caught. The chemistry between them zinged clear to the soles of his feet. "Like the two parts of the naupaka flower we belong together—forever. I'll never let you go."

Blonde hair haloed her head as she rested on a pillow. Through lowered lashes she gave him a come-hither look that made his pulse jump. Damn if she wasn't the sexiest woman he had ever laid eyes on. Then a moment of uncertainty peeked through her lust. He didn't give her the opportunity to refuse him, covering her with his body, her mouth with his.

Her lips were tentative against his. His tongue ached for the taste of her as he slipped inside. When she began to suck, pulling hard on his tongue, heat exploded between his thighs. Adrenaline rushed his brain as his desire swelled to every part of his body.

God, he loved her.

He smoothed his palm along her inner thigh. Velvet soft. His heart beat wildly the closer he got to the moisture he knew existed there. With his fingertips he stroked her moist slit. She was so wet. Her body quivered beneath his touch.

Was he dreaming? If so, he didn't want to ever wake up.

Nathan had waited so long to hold her again. He gritted his teeth to resist the orgasm that shot shards of sensation down his cock. On an exhale, he moved off her long enough to unbutton his jeans. In seconds he was naked and lying beside the woman he loved. She threw a leg over his thigh, and he rolled to his back as she straddled him. His throbbing erection lay nestled in the warmth of her sex.

"Is this really happening?" She pressed her palms against his chest. "Are you mine?" Once again uncertainty rose. "You won't leave me again?"

Dammit. The sorrow in her voice was enough to turn him inside out. Would he ever be able to make it up to her?

"Baby." He pulled her down so that their chests met. "I didn't want to let you go. I felt as if I didn't have a choice. I had to do the right thing."

She bit her bottom lip. Tears welled in her eyes. "I know, but—"

He hushed her with a tender kiss. "Please, can't we let this go?" he whispered against her mouth. "Nothing can keep us apart."

Chapter Four

Naked and straddling Nathan's hips, Paige knew it was too late to turn back now. If he left her after they made love tonight, she would drown in a pool of grief. No doubt in her mind existed that losing him again would kill her, but she was too weak to resist him. She wanted to feel him deep inside her body, wanted to believe he was truly hers.

When he rubbed against her wet folds, her mind spun. Fear and excitement collided to make every nerve in her body come alive. Her hold on his shoulders tightened.

With a tilt of her hips, the head of his cock breached her pussy. "Oh," she hummed. "Yes." She eased down, savoring every thick inch of him as he buried himself inside her. The emptiness she had carried with her the past five years was gone. The pressure against the very back of her sex sent a shiver of delight up her spine.

For several seconds, she didn't move. This was what she remembered. They fit perfectly together.

"S-so good," he muttered between clenched teeth. "Fist-tight." His eyes closed, as if savoring the warmth of her body surrounding him.

She smoothed her hand over his clean-shaven cheek. The love she felt for him surfaced so fast her heart fluttered.

Her hips slid forward and he grasped her waist. "E-easy,

baby." The tension on his face made her pause. Heavy-lidded, his eyes partially opened. "You have to remember, I've dreamt of this moment for five years. Let me enjoy the feel of you wrapped around me."

A lump formed in her throat, and she swallowed against it. Could it be true that he had suffered as much as she had?

Her tattered memories disappeared when his palms caressed a path to her breasts. He held them in his hands like they were fragile, something to cherish. His thumbs skimmed across the sensitive tips, once, twice, and then he squeezed.

Electricity streaked through her chest straight to her womb, tightening her sex. The need to rock against him was overpowering. She didn't know how much longer she could remain still. It became even more difficult when he leaned forward and wrapped his velvet mouth around one of her nipples.

He worked the peak with his teeth and tongue until she couldn't think of anything but the throb beating at her sex. Moisture released as tingles shot upward. Her hips moved of their own accord, back and forth, and then again.

"God you taste good," he muttered a second before he ensnared her other nipple, drawing it deep into his mouth. The suction made her mind go blank. Heat sizzled between her thighs.

"Nathan." She licked her parched lips and arched into his touch. All she could think of was him sucking harder. His teeth scraped across her tender skin, and a mixture of pleasure and pain shot to the depths of her pussy. Her clit began to throb, begging for the same attention.

As if he'd read her mind, he flipped her upon the bed and hovered over her. She reached for his arms and felt strength beneath her hold.

A sexy growl surfaced from deep in his chest. With a knee he wedged her legs farther apart. A single thrust parted her folds and his cock buried deep inside her again. Slow, sensual caresses teased her. She twisted her hips, raising them to meet each advance. Pressure built behind her clit, making her body ache for fulfillment. When her inner muscles squeezed, she bore down to increase the incredible sensation. Liquid fire bathed the walls of her pussy with each stroke.

Sexual hunger rose from someplace deep in her soul. It gnawed at every part of her being. A raspy moan pushed between her lips. This was what she'd missed in her life, the connection between two people so raw and passionate for each other that it crossed all barriers, transcended time and space.

"Nathan." His name was a desperate cry. Her head pressed back into the pillow. Every muscle in her body tensed as mindless pleasure built with alarming speed.

"Hold on, baby." He pulled her hands above her head, pinning her so she couldn't touch him.

Unable to feel his body drove her wild. "I need to touch you."

"So tight. Wet." His pace quickened and so did the desire to feel him beneath her palms.

The sound of flesh slapping flesh sent her senses careening with rapture. She arched into him, closing her eyes. Fire and ice exploded across her skin as stars burst behind her eyelids. "Nathan!" Red hot, her climax ignited, singeing every inch of her body. She bucked, convulsed and then she shivered. She couldn't hold still as one after another, spasms released. Nathan's cock swelled and jerked to send another stream of electricity throughout her body. When she looked at him, he stared at her with dark, penetrating eyes full of lust and, yes, love.

His arms trembled. Strong hands grasped her knees, parting her wider as he knelt between her legs and raised her hips. "Paige." His expression revealed he wanted to say more, but didn't. Instead he thrust, driving so deep inside her she gasped. Grinding his hips against her center, he rubbed her clit over and over again. "God," he groaned.

When the throb between her thighs started anew, she curled her fingers into the comforter. Her inner muscles clamped down on his erection and sucked eagerly to take him deeper and hold him there forever.

His nostrils flared. "Fuck." A rumble vibrated in his chest. There was something almost animalistic about the growl, making heat rise across her skin. She licked her lips slowly and his pupils darkened even more.

"Mine," he said so adamantly that she could almost believe it. The possessiveness in his voice thrilled her, stoked the fire inside her higher and hotter. Her stomach clenched. The pulse between her legs strengthened. She slid her fingertips through his dark chest hair and over his taut nipples.

"Come for me, baby." He spread her wider until it was almost painful. His thrusts became violent, hard and deep lunges, as he rammed into her again and again. "Let me hear you scream."

Paige whimpered. She didn't know how much more she could take perched on the edge of another climax. A conflagration in the center of her sex tightened, threatening to erupt.

His hands firmed. The muscles in his thighs grew taut. "That's it, baby." His voice was coarse. Then he threw back his head and roared. Hot spurts of come bathed her walls to trigger her orgasm.

A cry clawed up her throat and released. She arched her

back and jerked with each spasm that rippled through her, thrashing uncontrollably beneath him. Soaring high, she fought to hold onto the moment, relishing the way her body spun out of control. All too soon it was over and she felt herself drifting off the cloud of ecstasy.

The grip on her legs loosened as he guided them down on the bed, before he collapsed atop her. His breaths were short airy pants, matching hers.

Desperately, she wrapped her arms around him as if her hold would stop him from leaving her. She almost blurted, *I love you,* but she didn't speak the words. Instead, she pressed her face into the hollow of his neck and shoulder and inhaled the scent of his masculine heat. Prayed that he meant what he said earlier.

His fingers slid between the bed and the nape of her neck. He raised her head to meet him halfway and kissed her. It was a soft, gentle caress that touched her heart. "Thank you." She was about to ask for what when he added, "For believing in me. Letting me back into your life."

But that was the problem. Although she had given him her body, her heart, he didn't have her trust. She didn't know if there would be a day that she could forget about the past and give herself fully to him, but she knew she had to try.

"I have a surprise for you."

Oh no. She didn't know if she could take any more surprises.

He scooted off the bed and extended his hand to her. She took it willingly, and he helped her off the bed. The sweet aroma of their loving filled the room. On quiet footsteps, he slid open the large glass doors that led to the veranda. It had stopped raining, but the gray clouds remained, making the day gloomy. She inhaled the clean scent and the smell of the wet wood that was cool beneath her feet. He led her to the Jacuzzi. Water churned and beautiful orchids adorned the surface.

"When did you do this?" she asked.

He crossed the balcony to the bar. "Last night." From the small refrigerator he extracted a bottle of champagne and two flutes. He retrieved a corkscrew and inserted it into the bottle. Each twist resulted in a sharp grinding sound, and then a delightful pop ensued. The wine bubbled up, spilling over the rim. He shook his hand off, before pouring the effervescent wine into the glasses. The bottle clinked against the bar counter as he set it down and picked up the glasses.

"Isn't it a little too early for alcohol?" she asked.

He handed her a drink. "It's almost noon and we deserve it." He raised his glass. "To us and a long life together."

She tipped the rim of her glass to his and prayed that she had heard him correctly. Bubbles tickled her nose as she took a drink. She coughed and he smiled. It had been a long time since she had sipped champagne. Five years.

Together they walked toward the Jacuzzi. She climbed the steps and placed a foot into the warm water. The minute she eased down into its depth she released a sigh. After one more sip, she set the glass on the side. Nathan followed to take a seat beside her. Not even a heartbeat passed before he gathered her into his arms. She rested her head against his chest. He kissed her softly on the forehead.

The moment of silence lingering between them wasn't awkward. They had always had the uncanny ability to bask in each other's company without a word. She stared out into the gray and gloomy sky, listening to the ocean lick the shore. In the distance, a bird screeched. She snuggled closer and he held her tighter.

The moment was serene, peaceful, and she began to relax.

Nathan looked down at Paige and couldn't help smiling. She had fallen asleep. "Poor baby."

Easing her from his lap, he stood and carefully raised her into his arms. Water beaded and rolled off her silky skin. A gust of wind swept across the balcony. He held her closer, attempting to block the chill in the late-morning air. As he carried her into the cottage, Paige whimpered, but didn't wake. Quietly, he moved across the living room to the bedroom and then the bathroom. It was difficult, but he managed to jerk a towel off the rack and toss it over her, before he made his way back into the bedroom. She didn't stir as he laid her upon the bed. With a dab here, one there, he attempted to dry her off without disturbing her. When he was satisfied, he rolled her to her right side and eased the comforter and sheet from beneath her. Quickly, he dried himself and then crawled in to spoon her back and pull a sheet over them. For a moment he was overwhelmed, choked up with emotion. He had missed this. He fought to push the regret away. Those lonely days were gone.

Up to now Cami had been the only bright thing in his life. He gazed out the window. The rain had started again, but it was a light drizzle in comparison to the torrent that had hit earlier. Paige and he had made it over this first hurdle in their lives, but he wasn't a fool.

The fact was Paige and he lived two different lives. His was an easy living that his family's money allowed, something he and Paige had refused to consider five years ago. While she had continued on the path they had agreed upon by establishing a life and a medical practice, he had done a one-eighty, tossing his architectural dream to the wind.

Would Paige be willing to give up her practice? Move to Kauai? By purchasing the resort, the cottage where he and

Paige's love had grown that summer, he had promised his parents to join the family business. It had been a small price to pay to hold onto something he and Paige had shared together. He just hoped she understood why he couldn't let his mom and dad down now.

Paige moaned and he drew her closer.

While he held her, little details kept popping into his mind. Cami and Paige had already met. It wouldn't take them long to establish a relationship, one he was sure his ex would do her best to destroy. The damn woman hadn't let a day go by without throwing his feelings for Paige into his face. Marrying Sylvia had been wrong from the beginning.

He wedged a leg between Paige's, before kissing her shoulder.

Guilt invaded his thoughts. He had asked Janis to take Cami to visit his parents if there was a break in the weather. It would give him and Paige time to get reacquainted and discuss the particulars of their lives together. Cami and Janis enjoyed Lotus Point. His family had every conceivable amenity two girls could ask for. Yet his decision had been selfish. He couldn't stand the thought of being away from Paige for even a moment. He moved his hand to cup a breast and she didn't stir.

Would she like Janis? The young girl was more than a nanny—she was part of their family. She had been with them since Cami was born. He could still remember the argument he and Sylvia had when he hired Janis. She had no home, had been left here by a boyfriend who followed the waves, and the most important aspect was that she was good with children, like Paige.

He inhaled the scent of her skin and released a sigh. This was where he belonged, wrapped in her arms forever.

Paige woke to an empty bed in a dimly lit room. Had it been a dream? A silent cry rose in her throat, dying when the bedroom door opened. Light silhouetted Nathan's frame. She sucked in the breath she'd held at bay.

He carried a tray in his hands. "Evening, sleepyhead." He set the tray down on the small table in the room.

She rubbed her eyes. "How long was I asleep?" As if she sported a hangover, her head began to pound. He slid the glass doors of the bedroom open and a gush of salty air swept through the room.

"About eight hours." He walked back to the table and began to uncover the plates. The juicy scent of roasted meat met her nose. Her stomach growled. It seemed like forever since she had eaten.

She pushed into a sitting position and stretched. "I can't believe that." Her body felt deliciously sore. "I don't remember when I've ever slept that long. Have you been here all this time?"

"Yes." He poured wine into two glasses.

"Doing what?" she asked.

"Watching you. Did you know you snore?"

She huffed. "I do not."

"Do too. And you talk in your sleep."

She had never talked in her sleep. "Oh yeah? What did I say?"

Dressed in a white robe that matched hers, he strolled sensually to the bed and picked up her hand. He pressed his lips against her wrist. "You said you love me." He gave her hand a gentle pull until she stood before him. He reached past her to retrieve her robe and held it out for her to slip her arms through. "Hungry?"

"A little."

"Good." He secured her sash.

"Is this what life together will be like, you waiting on me?" she teased.

"If I have any say about it, yes." He winked, making her heart flutter. "Now eat."

Baked potato, steak and a medley of vegetables made her mouth water. Her knife sliced through the meat like it was butter. She couldn't wait to taste it as she forked a piece and placed it in her mouth. "Oh my God. This is almost orgasmic."

He laughed. "Orgasmic? I think I've been insulted."

She sliced another piece of steak and ate it without pause.

"You know my family owns this cottage." He took a sip of his wine. "I manage the resort now."

Her fork stopped midway to her mouth. "Really?" She set the utensil on the table. "What about your dreams of designing buildings?" It had been all he talked about when they were together. He'd wanted nothing to do with the family business. In fact, they had agreed to make it on their own without his inheritance.

"I encouraged Mom and Dad to purchase the resort after we—" He looked down at his plate, before raising his gaze to meet hers. "I mean, after we, um—"

"Split up," she finished his sentence. Yes, it hurt, but it was what it was.

"I had to have something that was ours."

Was that the real reason or had Sylvia demanded it? Paige was sure the simple lifestyle that she and Nathan had sought wouldn't measure up to his ex's standards. It hurt to think he might be lying to her.

For the next couple of minutes they ate in silence.

"Paige."

She looked up from the vegetables she pushed around her plate. "Yes?" The pause that followed put her on edge.

Nathan swallowed hard. "I owe it to my parents to continue managing this property. Not to mention it's the only home Cami has ever known."

Paige wasn't quite sure where this conversation was going, but it didn't have a good feel to it. "Nathan, what are you trying to say?"

"Would you be willing to relocate your practice to Kauai or one of the other islands nearby? I can't let my parents down. They're counting on me."

Oh Lord. Everything had happened so quickly she hadn't even given thought to their living arrangements. Did he have any idea of the time and effort she had dedicated to building her business? Her life in Denver?

"Paige?"

She glanced up at him, unaware she had even looked away. The vein in his forehead bulged, revealing his unease as he awaited an answer she didn't have. "I don't know."

"What does that mean?" he asked.

The weight on her chest returned with a vengeance. Nothing came without a price. Was her independence, her life in Denver, the practice she had nurtured from infancy, the price she would pay to be with Nathan? What guarantees were there that he wouldn't walk out on her again if the road got rocky? What would happen if Cami and she didn't hit it off? Would Nathan cast her aside for his daughter?

"Maybe." Self-doubt made her hesitate. "We've moved too fast." Paige couldn't believe her own words.

He shot up from his chair and came around to pull her off

her chair and into his arms. "Don't say that." He pressed their bodies together. "We'll find a compromise. Just promise me you won't pull away from me."

"I can't make that promise," spilled from her mouth, shocking even her.

"Dammit, Paige." He gave her a little shake. "I can't live without you. Please don't ask me to." Anxiety rose in his voice.

The choice to move and join Nathan should have been easy. He was all she had ever wanted, but she had lost in this game of love before. She had to be wise, guard her heart and take it slow. Didn't she?

All thoughts of taking it slow vanished when his lips met hers. She tasted his despair that quickly changed into sexual hunger when he unfastened her robe. As the soft material slid off her body she prayed she wasn't falling into the flames.

"Let me take you to bed and make love to you," he whispered against her lips.

"Sex won't solve our problems. We should talk before we go any further." She spoke the right words, though her body began to simmer with the warmth of his hands on her waist.

"Not tonight, Paige. I don't want to deal with this now. I can't. I need you. Now."

It was stupid. She knew it was stupid, but when he said it that way there was no way she could refuse him. Nor did she want to face the possibility of losing him once again. Besides, he was right. There would be another time to address their issues, but not now. She pressed her mouth to his. Tonight was for loving.

Chapter Five

Dressed in a tank top and a pair of board shorts, Nathan stepped onto the balcony and inhaled. "There's a break in the weather."

From where she lay on the bed she could see the gray sky, but patches of blue and the sun shone through. The scent of rain was gone, allowing the exotic aroma of the island to sweep in and caress her. She pushed into a sitting position, and the sheet slid down to expose her breasts.

Between lovemaking they had talked some more, but never came to an agreement. She truly understood where he was coming from with the promise he had made to his parents and Cami, but he had also made a promise to her. Try as she might she couldn't shake free of the insecurity or the need to hold on to the only thing that made her feel safe—her career and her home.

Swinging her feet over the edge of the bed, she stood and strolled toward him. She weaved her arms around his waist and pressed her body to his to rest her cheek on his back. The gentle hum of his breathing lulled her into a false sense of security almost as much as the waves rolling against the shore.

He glanced over a shoulder. His crooked smile made her heart skip a beat. "You're beautiful in the morning."

"And you're full of crap."

He turned in her arms and his head lowered. She placed a palm between their lips to evade his kiss. "Morning breath." In fact, her mouth tasted as if an army had marched through it. The most delightful chuckle met her frown as she lowered her hand.

"Go brush your teeth." He popped her on the ass and she yipped. "I thought breakfast on the balcony would be nice." While he stepped back into the bedroom to retrieve the tray, she remained behind to enjoy the gorgeous panorama.

Dammit. She had missed the sunrise as it kissed the horizon. No place on earth compared to Hawaii's beautiful sunrises and sunsets. In the nearby fronds of a palm tree she heard the sweet melody of a native songbird. It seemed to keep time with the waves below.

She sighed. "There's something magical about this place."

"There's something magical about you."

She pivoted to see him watching her. There was no denying the love that reflected back at her, which set off butterfly wings in her belly.

"Do you have any idea how beautiful you are naked with the ocean and blue skies as your backdrop?"

Goose bumps rose across her arms and legs. What did a girl say to words as lovely as his? "It would be an even better picture if you were naked beside me."

Deep, sexy laughter spilled from his lips. "You just want me to fuck you again."

She cocked her head to one side. "The thought did cross my mind." Her nipples beaded, the small change not going unnoticed as his gaze darkened.

His chin lowered. He curled an index finger, beckoning her to him.

Playing hard to get never entered her mind. No hesitation existed in her footsteps as she closed the distance between them and walked into his opened arms. She rubbed against him teasingly.

"Did I ever tell you how sensual your hard nipples feel against my chest?" he whispered close to her ear.

"No." She slid her body along his once more.

Oh yeah. That did feel good—real good. Her peaks tightened, breasts heavy with desire.

His hand smoothed down to rest in the small of her back, and a finger slid between the crest of her cheeks. He moved lower and a shiver raced up her spine. She liked where this was going, but first things first.

A step backwards and she pulled from his arms. "Be right back."

She dashed into the bathroom. It took only a couple of minutes for her to freshen up. She ran her tongue across the front of her teeth, tasting the minty flavor, before she walked back to the bedroom.

To her surprise and pleasure Nathan was stark-ass naked and sprawled across the bed. His hands rested behind his head, legs slightly parted. His impressive cock arched, hard and erect, toward his bellybutton. The picture of him lying there in wait could be featured in a centerfold, he looked so damn delicious. Five years had honed his body. Every line was defined, power and strength in each muscle.

"I thought maybe breakfast could wait." His smoky voice was all she needed to ignite the flame inside.

With each step that familiar drawing sensation splintered at her nipples and stung unmercifully. Moisture dampened her thighs. Adding to the excitement were the open glass doors. The voyeur aspect came in to play, making her desire heighten and her body burn. Just the thought of someone watching was exhilarating. One knee rested on the bed as she looked into his dreamy eyes, and then she paused.

What the hell was she doing? One more day with Nathan and she would sell her soul to be with him forever.

"Don't pull away from me."

She closed her eyes for a moment to gather her composure. "I'm scared," she admitted without shame. Truth was she couldn't let go of her independence. Five years ago she had had stars in her eyes. Today she was older, wiser. She couldn't just throw her life away, even for Nathan.

"I'm scared too, baby." He approached.

An outstretched hand kept him at bay. "Please don't." If he touched her she would lose control. She had never been able to resist his caress. "Why can't you and Cami come live with me? I'm sure your parents would understand." A tremor shook her voice.

"Think of what you're asking of me. Kauai is Cami's home— my home. She loves it here. Paige, I made a promise to my folks to help run the family business. This is my life now. Our life. Together."

"What I'm asking of *you*?" Paige shook with disbelief. Her hands balled into fists to contain her anger. "What happened to you, Nathan? Your dreams of becoming an architect?" She released a huff of dismay. "Even our agreement to not use your family ties or money has fallen by the wayside." Had that request been an unrealistic goal or had he slipped into whatever was easy once she was out of his life?

He looked away. "Things change, Paige."

The air in her lungs rushed out. "That's exactly my point. Everything has changed. You. Me. Our situations." She wrung her hands. "We're fooling ourselves to think we can pick up where we left off. There are too many differences between us."

He ran his fingers through his wavy dark hair. "Don't do this to us." He eased off the bed, stood and began to move toward her.

"Me?" She choked on the word. None of this had been her doing. Paige wanted nothing more in this world than to be with him forever. The sting of tears followed a wave of heat that burned across her face. "I'm so upset with you," she growled, the gravelly sound pushed from deep in her diaphragm. "I could just slap the shit out of you. This isn't my fault." She wasn't a violent person, but at the moment she felt like hitting something or someone, preferably Nathan.

He reached for her.

She pulled back her hand and released.

Crack.

Relief and guilt slammed into her, stealing her breath. Her palm stung as her eyes widened in surprise. "Oh my God." She covered her mouth with her hands. What had she done?

He rubbed his reddened cheek. "Feel better?"

Yes. No. Fuck.

Paige didn't know what she felt or for that matter how to feel. With the back of her hand she wiped at tears that sprung from out of nowhere. She had never hurt another human being, especially one she loved, and she did love Nathan with all her heart. Time and distance hadn't changed their connection. It was asinine to admit anything different, but she wasn't a fool. How could things work out between them?

He seesawed his jaw. "That's quite a right you have." His crooked smile rose.

Her hand fell to her side. "I'm so sorry. I don't know what came over me."

"It's okay." His warm palms slid up her bare arms. "Baby, I deserved it."

Yes, he did, but it didn't take away her self-reproach. She had hit him. A shudder shook her entire body.

"I know we have unanswered questions, but give us this holiday to work things out."

Paige knew she should get her clothes on and walk out the door, but her heart kept her rooted before him. "Nathan, I won't survive losing you again if we can't come to an agreement." There was no shame in her avowal, only the truth.

He dipped a finger beneath her chin. Their gazes met. "I'll never leave you. Maybe I can fly back and forth between Denver and Kauai." Even as he offered the suggestion she could see doubt in his worried expression. "I don't know what the answer is, but give me this holiday to work things out." He pulled her close.

Skin to skin, it felt so right in his embrace. She looked up at him, and he captured her lips in a tender kiss. Before she realized what she was doing, she slid her arms around his neck and tilted her head to deepen the caress. She had been wrong, she *was* a fool. But who could blame her? His sensual kiss was hard to resist.

Nathan moved his mouth over hers, so feather-light her lips tingled. "Is that a yes?" His arms tightened around her as if he had no plans to release her regardless of her response.

Talk about playing with fire. What he requested of her, she was helpless to oppose, even if she tried to fight it tooth and nail. Paige knew she couldn't walk away and it was tearing her up inside. The fact was both of them knew that with the break in the weather the airport had opened, perhaps not to Fiji, but she could return home.

"You'll stay throughout the holiday?" A hopeful note rose in his voice.

A small utterance in the back of her mind urged her to leave before it was too late. Still, she found herself nodding in agreement.

The biggest grin spread across his face. "Baby, I'm going to love you so thoroughly you'll never want to leave me."

Without a doubt she knew he could accomplish just that. They had never had a problem in that department—it was all the other outside influences. Like Cami. What would his daughter say about a new woman in their lives?

The troubled thought flew out of Paige's head when his palms slid down her back and he cupped her ass, pulling her cheeks apart. He nibbled on her neck. She leaned her head to the right to give him more access.

He eased back so their gazes met again. "You taste so good I could eat you." The fire that flickered in the depths of his eyes was bewitching.

Damn him. The man had a way of taking her from cool to blazing hot with just a look. Her breasts ached with desire, heavy and needy. Moisture dampened her naked thighs, setting off a throb she couldn't ignore. When his hips moved against hers, she glanced at his rigid cock and her mouth began to water. The memory of the first time she went down on him materialized in her head. He had lost control, screamed her name. Would his reaction be the same if she took him now?

Pleasuring him was the only thing on her mind. She guided him backwards to the bed. With a gentle shove, he fell upon the crumpled sheets and scooted toward the pillows. Resting back on his elbows, he flashed a glimmer of male satisfaction that she found incredibly sensual. Moisture dampened the apex of her sex. Slowly, she crawled upon the bed. He spread his legs wider. She licked her lips and he inhaled sharply. When she slipped between his thighs, lowering her body so that her chest touched the cool linens, a chill raced across her skin. She smiled up at him and blew warm air over his erection.

His hand speared through her hair. With a gentle nudge, he dragged her head down until her lips touched his engorged flesh. "Oh yeah, baby. Fuck me with that pretty mouth."

She cupped his balls and massaged them through her fingers, loving the feel of them sliding back and forth in their sac. Again she blew a warm stream of air on his genitals. The raging hunger in his eyes was all the encouragement she needed to part her lips.

As she drew her tongue up his shaft, he threw back his head. "Dear God!" His fingers curled, lightly pulling her hair.

Like a lollipop she tongued him, up one side, down the other, and finally made a swirling motion around the crown. He thrust and several inches of his thick erection filled her mouth. She lapped at the salty precome, running her tongue over the small slit.

He tasted so good.

Releasing his balls, she circled the base of his erection with her fingers and squeezed. A groan surfaced from somewhere deep in his throat.

"Your mouth is so hot." He raised his hips and another inch disappeared between her lips. His gaze was fixed on the place where they came together. "Fucking hot." The words were forced through clenched teeth.

Alternating from slow to fast to slow again, she worked her mouth over him, sometimes using her tongue, other times skimming his flesh lightly with her teeth. At times she simply focused on stroking the sensitive little spot just beneath the head of his cock. He seemed to really enjoy that.

"Sonofabitch, that's incredible."

She ignored his curse while she licked and sucked. In unison, she slowly slid her hand up and down his shaft. The terse sounds he made drawing air through clenched teeth only made her want to pleasure him more. A stream of semen bathed the back of her throat. He jerked as she swallowed.

"Paige. No." He eased back, withdrawing his hips. A little pop sounded as his cock exited her mouth.

Confused, she gazed up at him. Her tongue slid between her lips, savoring his taste.

He plopped his head down on the pillow and inhaled a ragged breath. "Oh sweet Jesus, don't do that." Beneath her hands, she felt the shiver that raced through him.

She moved over his body to blanket his hips with hers. He gripped her waist, holding her still. His hardness jerked against his belly. "Something wrong?"

"No." He pulled her down so they were chest to chest, hip to hip. "I don't want it to end so soon."

A quiet moment elapsed between them. Both of their hearts were pounding, their skin moist with perspiration.

"Remember that boat?" A mischievous grin rose across his face.

Heat flared across hers. How could she forget?

"Such a pretty blush." He stroked her ass. "You do remember."

Oh yeah. She remembered. He had told her the boat was too far away for its occupants to see as he took her against the railing on the balcony.

Liar.

When she climaxed, the boat's damn horn had blared for at least five minutes.

"How 'bout we recreate that moment, but with a twist."

"A twist," she repeated, not sure she liked the dark sensuality in his voice.

He nodded slowly. He stared at her with such intensity it was almost scary.

"Instead of me taking you here..." he caressed the wet slit of her pussy, "...I'll take you here." His fingertips nudged the tight skin of her anus. She knew he was waiting for a reaction and he got it.

She couldn't hide her surprise, even if she tried. Her eyes widened and her jaw dropped. In fact, she trembled. The forbidden thought sent her senses whirling. "I don't know. Will it hurt?"

Will it hurt? Duh. She was a doctor. Yes, there would be discomfort, but then again the sensitive nerves in that region could make for an incredible experience if done right.

"Not if you're prepared properly," he replied.

That meant lots of lube, and she meant a lot. She dragged in a taut breath. "Okay."

One of those animalistic growls rumbled in his chest. "You're amazing." He pulled her the rest of the way up his body and captured her mouth with his. She tasted his hunger, his excitement.

If they were starting anew, why not explore their desires with something fresh and erotic? She just hoped in the end she wouldn't regret it.

Paige anticipated his touch to be amorous and wild, but instead he held her tenderly while he nibbled on her bottom lip. Slanting his mouth, he moved leisurely over hers as he sipped from her lips. His fingers slipped between their bodies to find the spot that ached for his touch. When he caressed her clit, shivers slithered up her back. With long strokes he began to rub back and forth.

The heat in her body soared. Moisture released between her thighs. He pushed between her folds to stoke the flame even higher. Slick with her juices, he slid his fingers across her puckered skin, nudged gently with his knuckle.

Her brows rose.

He smiled reassuringly as he played around the sensitive area. Over and over, he withdrew his touch to enhance her anticipation and then returned, increasing the pressure each time to make her gasp and, yes, long for more.

"Oh God." She didn't expect to have such a reaction, but damned if her pussy didn't clench and release another flood of moisture. She wasn't aware of what his other hand was doing until it joined the party, and cool gel took the place of his knuckle.

Was the lube hidden beneath his pillow? What a rat. He'd had this planned all along.

She didn't have time to ponder the thought as a well-oiled finger breached her anus. Air pushed from her lungs. A little sting, but not the pain she had expected. Carefully, he worked the digit in and out, allowing her body to adjust. He withdrew and there was an emptiness she hadn't expected. He added another application of gel before inserting two fingers this time.

Words could not describe the fullness she felt or the thrill pulsing through her core. With each thrust she found herself moving against him, wanting more—needing to have his cock fill her the way his fingers did.

The scissoring effect he made with his fingers stretched her even more. When he inserted another finger, she welcomed his hand, needing to feel him deep inside her.

"I think you're ready." He reached beneath his pillow and exposed the tube of lube. She was too aroused to care. "Shall we adjourn to the deck?"

Her legs felt like rubber as he helped her from the bed and led her outside. All she could think of was easing the throb that vibrated between her thighs.

He positioned her a foot away from the wrought-iron fencing looking over the crystal blue ocean. White caps formed and disappeared as others took their places. Another storm approached, or was it the tempest threatening to sweep through her that made her heart beat faster?

He moved up behind her and her pulse started to race. "Lean over and take hold of the railing."

The wrought iron was cool as she wrapped her fingers around it. The reality that she couldn't see what he was doing was beyond arousing. When a boat moved into her view, chills slithered up her spine. Not again. "Nathan?"

"They can't see us." But he'd made that promise once before.

She was about to object when he bent his knees and thrust. His cock slid easily between the moist lips of her pussy. Her back arched and he pushed all the way in. The breeze that tossed the palm fronds and leaves of an orchid tree caressed her nipples and blew her hair around her shoulders and face.

He withdrew and then plunged forward again and again, each time a little firmer, a little deeper. As he stepped back, he withdrew completely.

"No. Please." Her plea was a mere whimper.

"Patience, baby. I just need to add more lube."

Her pussy clenched at the thought of the cool gel, of his cock parting her cheeks and delving deep.

"I can't wait to feel that sweet, sweet ass of yours."

One more coat of gel on his cock and Nathan moved up

behind her. He had never seen anything as sexy as Paige grasping the railing, waiting for him to take her. The sweet curves of her ass made his erection jerk, his balls draw up tight.

She flinched when he touched her hip. Her uneasiness was obvious, but there was also excitement. It was in the way she rode his hand as he had fingered her. In fact, her actions had begged for more.

He placed his dick at the entrance of her pink, puckered skin and eased just the head inside. Her taut hole was well greased and she took him without resistance.

His heart drummed. He couldn't believe she would allow him to do this, but he thanked God that she did. It was something he had dreamt of—claiming every inch of her.

With one hand he grasped her hip. The fingers of his free hand wrapped around his shaft. Slowly he worked the head of his cock in and out of the tight space, careful not to go too far, too fast. He pushed a little deeper.

A hoarse sound vibrated in her throat. "Oh," she breathed.

"Easy, baby. Relax. This won't work if you don't relax." What was he saying? He was as tense as a virgin boy. Then again, this was new territory for both of them. "As I push in you're supposed to press out to me." He'd read that somewhere. "If you struggle, it will hurt." He released her hip and applied more lube. They'd have a slippery mess before he was done, but he was bound and determined not to hurt her.

"I'm okay." She said one thing, but her shaky arms revealed something entirely different. "Just do it. That boat is coming closer."

He would have chuckled, but he was so friggin' hot it was all he could do to move cautiously. "Breathe in, baby." He parted her cheeks and aligned himself. "Now breathe out."

74

When she did he pushed forward, this time breaching the first ring of resistance.

She released a startled cry and whimpered softly.

Lord, please don't let her cop out on him now. His teeth clenched. He didn't know if he could stop.

He waited until her body stopped shaking before he moved deeper, felt the resistance and pushed forward. Goddamn. She was tight. Not to mention, he had never experienced anything as erotic as watching his cock disappear between her ass cheeks, one agonizing inch at a time. Every muscle in his body strained to hold back, take it slow, while his mind demanded more, faster.

"Fuck." A strangled cry ripped from her diaphragm. She jerked and he thought she was calling it quits. Instead of pulling away, she pressed back against him, shoving his erection a little deeper. "Now. Nathan. Fuck me now."

Red-hot excitement sizzled through his veins. He never realized how exciting it was to hear her swear. His balls jerked, fire raced up his spine and he thrust the rest of the way in. Multiple sensations exploded throughout his body.

For a moment he couldn't move. Hell. What was he saying? He couldn't breathe. His chest tightened, the pressure so intense he thought he might be having a heart attack.

"Yes." This time her scream was a blend of pleasure and pain. She panted, short choppy breaths. Her back was bowed. Her hair covered her face so he couldn't see her expression. When she threw back her head and turned to look at him, he saw pure ecstasy in her eyes. "So thick. Hard. Please more."

More? Oh fuck yes. More he could give her.

He gave a deep, throaty growl and dug his fingers into her hips. Breathless, he withdrew and slammed into her. His balls slapped her flesh, music to his ears. He eased back one more time and thrust hard and fast, again and again, fucking her in earnest.

When the muscles in her ass clamped down, she moaned. That was all the catalyst he needed to send him spiraling through space with no parachute. Heat licked down his dick, sending a shiver through him. His entire body jerked with each pump of come.

He collapsed against her back, his hand finding the ache between her thighs. The minute he touched the bundle of nerves she lit up like the Fourth of July. Her body convulsed. She cried out in unison with the loud blare of the boat's horn.

Neither of them immediately reacted. Their energy spent, it took a couple more seconds to even care that they had been caught once again. When she found her voice, the cutest giggle he had ever heard slipped from her mouth.

"Sweet Jesus." Her laughter was breathy. "You've done it to me again."

Extracting himself from her beautiful body, he spun her around to press his lips to hers. The sultry kiss was the only way he could express everything he was feeling at the moment.

He loved this woman.

When the caress ended, he wrapped his arms around her. The horn was still blowing. The occupants of the watercraft were jumping up and down in celebration. "We must have given them quite a show."

Through sated eyes half-shuttered, she looked up at him. "Yes, I believe we did."

"Shall we?" he said with a chuckle and a wink.

"Why not."

At the same time they turned and waved to those watching, and then like two naughty children they ran into the bedroom laughing. They fell upon the bed in each other's arms, Paige on her back, while his chest half covered hers. He brushed the hair from her eyes. "I love you."

Her chortling died. She touched her fingertips to his face and traced the line of his jaw. "I love you too."

Wrapping her in his arms, he held her close. Kissed her like a man in love.

The tender sigh she released filled his chest with happiness. "Do you want to shower or eat first?"

"Shower." She pushed from his arms and off the bed to stand. Blowing him a kiss over her shoulder, she crossed the room.

He rolled to his side, propped a hand beneath his head and watched her sweet ass disappear into the bathroom. Crawling out of bed, he stood to follow. No way was she showering without him.

He headed toward the armoire that held the television and grabbed the remote to switch it on.

"Another storm is anticipated, arriving on the heels of the last. It should hit the islands by seven this evening," the weatherman announced.

He shook his head. "Dammit." They hadn't had this much rain in a while. He turned down the volume before walking to the desk and picking up the telephone. The phone beeped with each number he punched.

"Cross residence. This is Naomi."

"Hi, Mom. How's the girls?" The shower started and he looked toward the bathroom door. "And Cami's foot?"

"Safe and sound and she's doing fine."

"Janis is giving her the medicine?"

"Yes, Nathan. When will you be joining us? The Christmas

celebration will be starting soon."

"Uh. Mom. I wanted to talk to you about that."

"Why do I get the feeling I'm not going to like this?"

"Paige is in town."

There was a pregnant pause on the other end.

"Nathan Daniel. Do you know what you're doing?" She never called him by his first and middle name unless she was upset with him or the situation was serious.

"Mom, I love her. Five years didn't change that."

"And what about her? You know, sweetheart, people change."

"Not Paige." He found himself smiling. Yes, physically she had changed—time does that—but she was still the woman he had fallen in love with that summer.

"Just be careful. Will she be joining us for Christmas?"

"I hope so."

"Give her my love and we'll see both of you no later than Christmas Eve." Her voice held no room for discussion. No one argued with Naomi Cross, including him. He hung up the telephone and headed toward the bathroom.

The mirrors were cloudy with condensation. How could he forget she liked her water really hot? The shower was a wraparound, so he just walked in. She squeezed her hair and glanced over her shoulder. Her drop-dead smile pulled him to a stop.

How could one woman be so beautiful?

Water beaded off her skin and rolled to the marble floor to swirl around the drain and disappear. The delicate arch of her back, full breasts and an ass to die for didn't even compare to the beauty within. His parents had loved her immediately. Cami and Janis would too.

"Are you going to stand there staring at me?" she asked.

"Maybe." He joined her beneath the warm water—no make that hot. He didn't know how she enjoyed this.

"I need to go to town. I have no clothes and no money."

"Neither are issues." He pressed his wet body against her back. "I plan to keep you naked and dependent upon me."

She chuckled, wiggling her ass to breathe new life into his cock. He slid his palms upward to cup her breasts.

"No, really. I left my purse on the airplane. Both it and my luggage are enjoying themselves in Fiji with Mom and Susan."

He gave her nipples a pinch and then released them. So she wasn't meeting someone special in Fiji. He breathed a sigh of relief. "We better hurry then, because there's another storm heading in. But first..." he smoothed his hand down her abdomen, "...I think I'll wash you." Any reason to touch her again he'd take.

Chapter Six

Paige didn't remember Kauai being so windy. The palms swayed in the haughty breeze that snatched a hat from a tourist. He grabbed, but missed. What a sight watching him run down the street after it.

As they continued to drive through town she noted that none of the stores had goods on the sidewalks like they usually did. The town was missing the warm inviting atmosphere she remembered. Nathan had chosen to take her to Kukui Grove Shopping Center, the Garden Isle's largest and only regional mall.

"I promise the mall has everything a woman could want in a shopping experience. At least that's according to Cami and Janis. It's one-stop shopping. There are even two banks for you to choose from." It was the first time he had really spoken about his daughter.

"How is Cami doing?" Paige approached the subject cautiously.

"Good. She had a great doctor." He smiled and winked.

There were so many questions she wanted to ask, but she remained silent. Hidden away in the cottage, just the two of them, one could easily forget the real world. Soon they would have to face their conflicts and quit hiding beneath the covers, pretending their problems didn't exist. Still her body was deliciously sore.

He glanced over at her as he steered the Hummer into a parking place and stopped. "What's that grin for?"

"You."

"That's what I like to hear." He pulled her into his arms. "Did I happen to mention how amazing you were this morning?"

She gave him a quick peck on the lips. "About a million times." In reality, amazing didn't even begin to describe their time together. It had been explosive. She could still feel the effects of their loving every time she moved.

A gust of wind nearly drove her sideways as she and Nathan stepped out of the Hummer simultaneously. The breeze whipped around them, tugging at their hair and clothes as they dashed toward the mall. He opened the door and she ducked inside.

Once again she wore her sandals, jeans and T-shirt. It was that or the bathing suit or scrubs she'd found in the bag she had received from the hospital.

She looked outside the window at the thunderclouds that had choked out the sun. "It looks to be a bad storm."

"Yep. Looks like we will have to hunker down in the cottage."

She liked the sound of that.

"I talked to Mom today. She expects to see us Christmas Eve."

"Us?"

"Yes. Us." He kissed her lips. "You know Mom, so it's fruitless to argue with her."

Paige laid her cheek against his chest. All she had ever dreamt of was right before her. Did she dare grab it with both hands?

"Where to first?" he asked.

She pulled out of his embrace. "Bank."

"This way."

The list of things she needed seemed to grow as they strolled hand in hand. She had cancelled her credit cards over the telephone. The thousand dollars in her wallet could probably be kissed goodbye. Did the flight attendant still have her medical ID?

They entered the bank and a brassy-looking blonde yelled, "Nathan." She didn't waste any time coming to his side. She leaned in and kissed him on the cheek. Her cherry-red lipstick left a mark. "What brings you out in weather like this?" Her appraising gaze slid up and down Paige.

"The usual." He hesitated for only a moment. "Yolanda McDavid, this is Dr. Paige Weston."

"Doctor?" Yolanda's eyes brightened with awareness. "Oh my. You must be the one all the local chatter is about."

Paige wasn't sure she wanted to know what that meant, so she didn't comment. Still, she extended her hand to Yolanda. She doubted the woman had worked a real job in her life, judging by her silky-smooth hand, stylish dress and gold jewelry.

Yolanda scanned the immediate area. "Is Sylvia here?"

Nathan's backbone stiffened. "No. She's spending the holiday in New York, remember?"

"Oh. Of course, what a shame. I know Cami misses her mother terribly." The concern that spread across Yolanda's face appeared as artificial as the woman's busty chest. She released a heavy sigh. "Well, I must be off." This time when she pressed her lips to Nathan's cheek, leaving yet another print, Paige could have sworn she lingered longer than necessary. "It was a pleasure to meet you, Dr. Weston."

"Likewise." Paige didn't miss Nathan's frown as Yolanda walked away. He shook his head. "Just a guess." She took a tissue out of her pocket. "Friend of Sylvia's?" She dabbed at the lipstick on both his cheeks. The marks smeared, but she was able to wipe all traces of the other woman from his face.

"She's trouble," was all he would say.

Yolanda disappeared into the midst of shoppers attempting to cram their final purchases into the remaining three days before Christmas.

"Nathan, there's no need for you to hang around if you have more shopping to do."

"I think I'll stay here with you. Keep an eye on you from that chair over there." He gave her a kiss before turning and walking toward the seat, while Paige headed for an open teller. In no time she had more cash and traveler's checks then she could carry in her pocket.

It was time to shop.

Nathan joined her. "Get everything you needed?"

"Yes."

"Where to now?" he asked.

"Macy's." On the way a toyshop caught her attention. If she were to spend Christmas with the Crosses, she would need gifts. "What do you think I could get your daughter for Christmas?"

His eyes brightened. "That child has everything, but she does like dolls. It seems she can't get enough of them."

They strolled into the toyshop, and Nathan led her straight to the section with rows and rows of dolls. He picked up a porcelain doll with a velvet red dress. "She doesn't have this one."

Paige couldn't hide her surprise. "You know what dolls Cami owns?"

"Yes, and I make a badass cup of make-believe tea too."

She burst into laughter. His ability to not take himself too seriously was one of the things she had fallen in love with that summer. She'd lay a bet that he was a terrific father.

She instantly grew quiet. So much had transpired over the last five years. What if she and Nathan had changed so much that their life together wouldn't work out? She had established herself in Denver. She lived comfortably for the first time in her life. A single parent's paycheck never stretched far enough with two kids. Yet, all in all they had done okay after her father had abandoned them.

"You okay?" he asked.

"Yes." She forced a smile. Now wasn't the time to embellish on her concerns.

He carried the doll to the register, while she lagged behind, attempting to find her game face. She had to be back at work a week after New Year's. There were people and patients who depended on her, but that meant leaving Nathan behind. Her eyes watered as she paid for the doll.

Nathan shot a glance in her direction. His forehead furrowed, but he didn't speak. Instead he moved closer, snaking an arm around her shoulders. He only released her when the cashier handed the wrapped present to him.

Without a word they headed for Macy's.

The first thing Paige saw when she walked through the doors was the purses. She had plenty, but she did need something to carry her money. Of course, another purse never hurt anyone and she could use it when she got back home. The thought came so naturally. Home. The million-dollar question remained. When her time here ended would she return to her old life?

"Baby." He eased up behind her and wrapped his arms around her waist. "We'll work through this."

"Can we? Nathan, there's a whole body of water between us and that's just the miles between us. What about all the other things? You can't travel back and forth, and I've never made a badass cup of make-believe tea."

Nathan would have chuckled if the subject wasn't so serious. Paige was right. "Let's get what you need and go back home."

"But that's the point, Nathan. This isn't home, not for me." She lowered her voice. "It's a place were we left our memories five years ago." Her eyes grew misty. "We've just taken a short trip from reality to relive them." When she put it that way, the situation did have a bad ring to it.

Before he let her go, he placed his mouth next to her ear. "I won't let you go—I can't."

The doubt in her eyes was hard to miss. It nearly broke his heart. How would Cami feel about moving to Denver? Would Sylvia attempt to block the move? And what about his parents?

She snatched up a random purse and matching wallet. Without another word she walked straight to the checkout counter and plopped them on top. "I'll take these."

Neither of them spoke as she sought out the lingerie department. He had to admit feeling a little awkward surrounded by women's intimate wear. Yet when Paige began to make several bra and panty selections, he started to imagine what she would look like in them.

As they approached the nightwear, he chose a short see-through baby doll with a matching thong. He continued to walk along the racks, when a long slinky black satin gown caught his eye. The picture of it sliding over her curves, down her silky legs

85

to pool on the floor made his cock firm. He quickly grabbed the lingerie before moving on. His final selection was a lacy little cover-up.

"Are you finished?" Did he detect a chuckle in her voice?

He took the items she held in her hands and piled them with his on the counter. "I think this will do." When she tried to pay for them, he brushed her hand away. "This is on me."

Next stop was women's wear where he became a human hanger. He had never gone shopping with Sylvia and now he knew why. Paige tossed several T-shirts and spaghetti-strap tanks into his arms and even picked up a sexy little bikini and wrap for herself and one for Janis. Next were Christmas presents for his mother and father.

"What can I get you for Christmas?" she asked.

"Seeing you in that black nightgown on Christmas morning will be enough for me."

"No, really."

He would have taken her in his arms, but they were laden with packages and boxes as they walked through the aisles. "Paige, you're all I want. You're all I've ever wanted."

She gave him a weak smile. "Here, let me take some of those." He offloaded a couple light bags and they headed for the exit.

From the window he could see the storm had gotten worse. The sky was almost black. The wind hadn't died down, bending the trees like they were made of rubber. With little effort the door swung wide. The mall would be closing the stores down soon and that meant the restaurants as well.

"Would you like to pick something up for dinner or eat at home?" Like fingers, the breeze snatched at the packages he held. One bag ripped, but he kept everything intact as they hurried toward the car.

She didn't answer him until they were securely in the vehicle. "Either is fine." Her cheeks were pink, her hair windblown.

With a twist of the key, the engine roared to life. Just before she turned away and stared out the window, worry shone in her eyes.

Damn. He hated her insecurity, but who could blame her? He was asking her to leave her life behind to join him and Cami in Kauai. And there was still that trust issue they couldn't shake.

The wind was so bad he had to fight to keep the Hummer on the road.

"I know the cottage isn't home, Paige. The resort was an investment to my parents, but to me it was a little piece of our time together. I gave up my dream of a career to hold on to what we had." He placed a palm on her knee. "I still remember that first day I saw you. You were stretched out upon the beach, your bikini top undone as you sunbathed. I prayed that you'd roll over."

Did she smile?

Paige had just finished medical school. He had gone through a bad breakup with Sylvia.

"That night when you and your friends joined Bob and me at the cottage, I knew I'd found the woman of my dreams. Do you remember that evening? The stars. The moon. It was magical."

The tears in her eyes said that she remembered. "What happened, Nathan? I mean between you and Sylvia?"

He shrugged. "We were oil and water. You know I never loved her. Cami was the link between us. I'd do anything for her."

"You have full custody?"

He flinched. "Are you kidding? You think Sylvia would give up the leash she has around my neck?"

Paige's face hardened.

"Early in the marriage there was a part of me that wished I could love Sylvia and give Cami what she wanted most of all—a mother and a father. But you were always in the back of my mind." He released a heavy sigh.

"Why didn't you call, let me know what was happening?" Paige asked.

His laughter held no amusement. "You said you never wanted to see me again. You refused my calls. Hell, you changed your telephone number, even moved your practice." His gaze darted to her and then back to the road. "Didn't stop me. I googled you."

She chuckled. It was the first happy sound since their discussion had turned serious.

"Why haven't you married?" The question was bittersweet as he briefly dragged his sight back to the road. The thought of another man holding her had given him more than one night of restless slumber.

It was her turn to shrug. "Never found the right man."

"Is that the only reason?" he probed.

"No." She paused. "I never stopped loving you."

The knot developing in his throat grew to the size of a baseball. He steered the Hummer off the road and left the engine running. "Come here, baby."

She leaned over the console and he embraced her. "It's our time," he whispered. "Nothing will come between us this time." As he held her, big fat raindrops plopped on the windshield. It started slowly at first, steadily increasing until it ricocheted off the glass. "We'd better get going."

Driving was tough. Visibility was almost nonexistent. By the time they reached the cottage the weather had morphed into a torrential downpour. He had never seen it rain so fiercely in December.

"This is unbelievable," she said. "There's no way to get inside without getting drenched."

"True." He handed her the key to the cottage. Reaching into the backseat, he gathered up the bags, leaving the gift-wrapped presents behind. "Careful, the ground is slick."

In unison, they opened the vehicle's doors and got out. They were both laughing, soaked to the bone, as they stumbled into the house.

A kitchen light gave a soft hue to the room. Her shirt stuck to her chest, giving him a view of the lacy bra beneath. She tossed her hair back and water droplets released. There was something wild and sexy about the way she looked that sent his pulse racing. He released the grip he had on the bags and they fell to the floor.

One step brought him before her. She stared up at him and her laughter died. Their eyes met, hers suddenly filled with questions.

"So beautiful." He pushed the damp hair out of her eyes before smoothing his hand to the nape of her neck. Slowly he pulled her to him. Their lips touched. He moved his mouth over hers.

She hesitated as if she would deny him. "We should talk," she murmured.

"We will." He nudged her nose with his. "I promise." He nipped her bottom lip. "I need you now."

He knew the moment she surrendered. Her arms folded around his neck. Her mouth parted to his probing tongue and he dipped inside. She tasted sultry, of dark starry nights and a warm summer breeze. Long, slow kisses stoked the flame inside him until a tingle started in his groin.

She arched her neck.

He caressed the length, raining kisses along her tender skin to the hollow of her collarbone. The hunger to taste every inch of her body grew even stronger. With a tug, her shirt slipped to bare a shoulder. His lips found their way to the moist skin.

He trembled. "I need you naked."

Tonight he would make all her uncertainty disappear. Tonight he would bare his soul to keep her.

Chapter Seven

"I need you naked." Nathan's words rang in Paige's head. Strong hands buried beneath her shirt. Fingertips skimmed lightly across her abdomen, making her heart beat faster. "Please, baby."

How could she deny the longing in his voice or her own need that built with alarming speed?

They stood dripping wet just inside the door of the cottage. Scattered packages lay at their feet. Rain pelted the roof and windows. A flash of lightning illuminated the dim room followed by a loud clap of thunder that rattled the glass. While the weather kicked up its heels and raged, the world inside this small bungalow stood still.

Achingly slow, he pushed her T-shirt up to send goose bumps across her arms. It didn't help that the air currents from the overhead fan caressed her damp flesh.

She raised her arms and he slid the shirt over her head, stealing her sight. When she could see again she peered into eyes so dark with desire her heart skipped a beat.

There had always been an electrifying chemistry between them, a mutual sexual attraction that turned explosive each time they touched, but was it enough? Could they overcome the past and the present to carve out a future?

The catch of her bra popped free. Sensitive nipples drew

taut. She closed her eyes and savored the rays of sensation that played havoc with her peaks and quaked through her breasts. His fingertips smoothed ever-so-lightly across the very tips, and she wondered if the caresses might be her imagination. Her eyes remained closed, heightening the feel of his hands moving across her flesh like a feather to tease and tantalize.

"I love you so much." His deep, sensual voice slid over her skin to push her desire higher and higher. A flood of moisture released between her thighs. The spasm that came next felt sinfully delicious. "Soft." He made little circles around her nipples, igniting sparks of electricity that made her shiver with excitement.

When he wrapped his warm, wet tongue around the engorged bud, she sucked in a ragged breath. Fiery need shot south. Her pussy clenched and a moan pushed between her lips. She speared her fingers through his damp hair and held him to her breast, before she opened her eyes and glanced down. Her heartbeat went wild. She'd never seen anything as sensual as his heated expression as he suckled.

Taking the other nipple between his fingers, he pinched. Sweet, sweet pain exploded. "Nathan."

With mesmerizing blue eyes he looked up at her, and she melted inside. He released the hold on her breast. "What, baby?"

"Please." His touch had reduced her to begging, but she couldn't help it. Need clawed at her unmercifully. She had no willpower when it came to him.

"Do you want me to fuck you?" His naughty words matched his sexy grin.

The image of him buried deep inside her, thrusting in and out, their bodies locked together, made her groan. "Yes. I need you inside me." Another wave of moisture released between her thighs. She pulled at his T-shirt. "Off. Now."

But instead of pushing forward, he took a step backward and slipped his shirt off. "Are you hot for me?" Burying his fingertips into the waistband of her jeans, he tugged, dragging her so close his warm breath caressed her face when he spoke again. "How wet are you?" He didn't wait for her to answer. Instead he shoved his hand deeper and discovered for himself.

When his fingers caressed her slit, a shiver raced through her. Her legs parted on their own with a need for him to continue the glide of his hand across her slick folds.

"My God, baby. You do want me."

As he circled her clit she grabbed his biceps and held on. "Please, Nathan. I need you now."

Rain continued to ping off the roof. Another flash of lightning and burst of thunder followed on its heels. The overhead lighting in the kitchen flickered once, twice, before casting them in a veil of darkness, but that didn't deter them. If anything, the lack of sight heightened the moment with the mysterious lure it induced.

Paige's pulse stuttered and then sped when Nathan exerted pressure against her clit. Her inner muscles pulled tight. She shuddered. The delicious sensation lingered before dying slowly when he moved away. She inhaled and relaxed, waiting for his return. When he touched the bundle of nerves again, she rocked her hips back and forth, riding his hand. Seductive fingers worked her into a sexual frenzy.

She was ready, so ready. Her hand fell to the button of her jeans and she unfastened them. The zipper went next, falling with a whisper. She was about to push down her pants when he started to scoot his feet. They took little steps in the dark until the couch pressed against her knees. She sat, while Nathan moved the coffee table out of the way. Then he knelt before her.

Hands on her hips, he eased her jeans down. When she was naked, he tugged her legs to guide her hips off the couch. He supported her legs by draping them over his shoulders.

His soft growl sent chills up her spine.

Oh God. Yes.

Paige loved his cock deep inside her, but nothing compared to the raw intimacy of him going down on her. She craved the feeling of his mouth on her clit, licking and sucking, like he had done so many years ago. Just the thought of his tongue and lips teasing her pussy sent liquid heat surging through her veins.

The stream of warm air against her wet folds made her skin prickle. But he didn't touch her, almost as if he wanted to prolong her anticipation, and it was working. Add the ache low in her belly which was increasing with every second, and the thought of his touch was like a drug.

He sighed, the gentle timbre one of longing. "Damn, baby, I've missed you. I can't wait to wrap my tongue around those beautiful lips of yours." His tongue slid across her clit and she flinched, hips coming off the couch. "Sensitive?" He chuckled.

"Don't tease me, Nathan." She shuddered with the sensual pleasure streaking through her body. "Do me now."

That sexy rumble in his throat sent her senses reeling. Her fingers curled into the sofa. She couldn't wait much longer. The moment he flattened his tongue and smoothed it over the length of her slit, her mouth parted on a soft cry. A burst of tingles erupted in her core, shooting in all directions.

"Sweet," he hummed against her flesh. "Tastes so good."

With his wicked tongue he licked slowly around the engorged organ and fluttered over it once again. Every nerve ending jumped, raw and sensitive. Her heartbeat increased, her breaths short and quick pants. He parted her folds and a

94

throaty groan pushed from her lips.

As he fucked her with his mouth, she squirmed, loving the feel of his face buried against her core. He paused briefly to inhale her scent. "Mmm."

She trembled. "Nathan, please."

He lowered his head and once again began to ravish her. The sensual sounds he made lapping at her flesh drove her desire higher. Low and husky, his moans made her body vibrate with excitement. In and out he thrust, sipping at her juices. When he captured her nub in his mouth and sucked, her head fell back on a cry.

Blood rushed her tender folds, setting them to burn hotter. "Yes." Every caress was heightened. Even the whisper of his breath on her wet skin stoked the flame. Her breasts were full and swollen, her clit throbbed.

Nathan's loving was even better than Paige remembered.

She tightened her grip, fingers twining in his hair as she held him close. Her reaction had the most incredible effect on him. He jerked her forward and sucked even harder. His tongue went wild against her clit. The pressure was unreal, drowning her in white-hot pleasure that seared her body.

Her climax rose swiftly. Every muscle tensed. She writhed against him, his name a scream upon her lips. An inferno of heat spread like a wildfire from her core up her length to set her cheeks on fire. Her entire body shook as her release exploded.

Nathan didn't offer her a break. Through it all he unmercifully devoured her. Each stroke of his tongue, the suction of his mouth, pushed her closer to the edge of insanity.

A broken cry escaped her parted lips. "No more. Nathan." It was too intense.

"Please, baby. I don't want to stop. You make me ache for

more." The raspy plea in his voice was a sensual caress to her senses. "Do you have any idea how hot and sweet you taste?" He didn't wait for a response. Instead, he dipped his head and pushed his tongue along her slit, careful not to touch her pulsing nub.

"Nathan. I can't... Ohhh."

He licked a long, slow path against her skin, blowing softly on her wetness to steal her objection in a single gasp. Noninvasive strokes allowed her the time she needed to come down from one orgasm, before his tongue pressed more demandingly against her flesh. He parted her folds, delved deep to rekindle the heat between her thighs.

He played her like a fine instrument, strumming every chord to make her moan and writhe beneath his assault. Lightning lit up the room. The sight of him loving her, his head bobbing, sent her mind spiraling. Another climax broke on a clap of thunder that she felt throughout her entire body. Hot male groans washed over her. The fierce contractions of her womb stole her breath. One after another, the spasms clenched and released.

"Nathan. Oh my God." A light sheen of perspiration covered her brow, her skin felt alive, her insides a conflagration. Life without him had been hell. She didn't know until this moment just how much.

The storm continued to hammer the cottage to the rapid beat of Nathan's heart. His body hummed with desire. He could smell Paige's heat. Her sweet scent was an aphrodisiac that threatened to drive him insane if he didn't take her now. His cock ached, pulsing and throbbing beneath the restriction of his jeans. He removed her legs from his shoulders and pushed to his feet, while she scooted up into a sitting position on the couch.

Fast and shaky pants made her chest rise and fall rapidly. Shadows and light from the storm filtered over her beautiful face, giving her a mysterious air that thrilled him. She had come apart beneath his touch. Together they made music that no musician could compete with.

How had he ever gotten along without her?

"You're mine," he said firmly. He just had to make her believe it.

"I've always been yours." Her words tightened his chest. "I never stopped being yours or loving you."

Selfish bastard. While he had gone forward with his life to carve out a family for Cami, Paige had not. How badly had she suffered from his mistakes? Guilt slowed the progress of him removing his jeans.

Still, he hadn't lived a life without cost. Five miserable years of hell lying beside a woman who knew he loved another. It had been their undoing, so basically the failure in their marriage had been his fault. He had destroyed two women's lives.

"Nathan?" Paige's tender voice brought him back to the moment. "Are you going to finish what you started here?" Her laughter was light and airy.

His body burned for her, while his heart ached. As he pushed his jeans over his hips and past his legs, he wondered if he would ever be able to make it up to her. Thunder cracked, a flicker of lightning allowing him a brief look at her beautiful face flush with arousal. Before the brilliance died he reached for her. She stood and went willingly into his arms.

Her body was warm against the chill of his. Her heat went straight to his bones to fill him with the love her surrounding arms offered.

"I love you." His words came so naturally. "You have no idea how much."

She tipped her head up and he captured her lips, so soft next to his as he slanted his mouth across hers. When his tongue caressed the seam of her lips, she opened and he swept inside to taste her. No bitterness or anger or regret existed in her kiss, only the nectar of love and forgiveness for the errors of his ways. He didn't deserve her, but he would take what she offered.

What started out tender quickly turned fervent, a desperate need to right the wrong he'd done. His cock grew even harder, aching to feel her snug around him. He thrust his tongue in and out of her mouth, mimicking the rhythm of his hips against hers. She whimpered beneath his assault as their tongues dueled for control. He couldn't get enough of her—never would.

"I need you now." Her heart beat against his chest. "Nathan, please."

He loved it when she begged for him to take her. "How do you want me, baby?"

"In the bed, on the couch or table or floor..." she slid her silky body up and down his, sending his arousal skyrocketing, "...against the wall. I want it all." Her hands moved restlessly across his skin, setting off white-hot sparks wherever she caressed.

A smile of male satisfaction crept across his face. They had christened every place in this small cottage that summer so many years ago. They had plenty of time to reenact the warm, lazy days and savory nights spent together, starting now.

He shuffled his feet, guiding her away from the sofa. Electricity zinged between them when he pinned her against the wall. She mewled, the soft cry so arousing that he shoved his hands beneath her knees to raise her legs. Parting her thighs, he spread her wide and moved between them. So wet. So ready. Her warm pussy pressed against his cock. With an upward tilt of his hips, he slid between her moist folds, burying himself to the hilt.

She gasped and pushed against his shoulders, her head falling back against the wall with a thud. "You feel so good."

Her body surrounded him so tightly that blood roared to his groin. His sensitive balls drew taut. His hands moved from her legs and stroked down her back until he cupped the smooth globes of her ass. She locked her ankles around him, drawing him snug as he rocked against her sex. He squeezed her naked skin, his fingers flexing and gripping to part her rounded cheeks. The little squeal she released was so fucking hot.

"Harder," she demanded. "Take me hard and fast."

Hard and fast he could do, it was the slow and easy that would give him a problem tonight. Liquid fire surged throughout him with the sounds of moist, suckling flesh. The musky scent of their lovemaking filled his nostrils along with the soft feminine scent of Paige.

He loved her so much it hurt.

A hard blast of semen exploded through the small slit in his cock, ripping him asunder. He cried out as the ruthless pleasure/pain washed through him. Like a loud drum, his heartbeat filled his ears, nearly silencing her scream. Stars burst behind his eyelids. Each spasm of her precious pussy triggered another tremor, another jet of come. Her sweet muscles contracted and released, wringing every bit of energy from his now-listless body.

His head fell upon her shoulder. Breathing harsh, his body damp with perspiration, he couldn't think straight, didn't try as he attempted to rein in his control. Useless. Control around Paige was near to impossible. She had that much effect on him.

Her gentle hand brushed the hair from his eyes. He looked up and imagined he could see her love radiating in the darkness. He didn't need to see her blue eyes to know emotion was there—he felt it.

How did he come to be so lucky?

She pressed her lips against his. "Should we do something about the lights?"

"Lights?"

She chuckled softly. "Do we have any candles?"

He released her ass, and her legs drifted to the floor. "They're in the top shelf of the linen closet." He rubbed his cheek against hers. "I'll get them." He strolled across the room, only bumping into a chair once before locating the closet. Blindly, he felt for the candles and found a box of them, along with two in holders. He grabbed the crystal and moved his hand over the surface to locate matches. After he found them, he made his way through the darkened room to the table.

A hiss followed the path of the matchstick as he lit it. A blue flame flickered and the stifling odor of sulfur filled the room. When he had both candles lit, he noticed the two halves of the naupaka flowers pressed together as one. "Just as they should be," he whispered.

"What?" Paige asked, coming up behind him.

He picked up the flower and handed it to her. "The pieces are still connected."

She gazed upon the flower with something close to awe. "It's amazing."

"No. You're amazing." Everything about her was extraordinary. From the young woman he had fallen in love with to the confident woman who stood before him. She saved lives, including his. "Come here."

She set the flower on the table and stepped into his waiting arms. With a finger beneath her chin, he raised her gaze to meet his. Candlelight danced in her eyes. He lowered his head and captured her lips for a long, slow kiss. When the caress ended he held her close, savoring the moment.

"Do you know what I'd like?" she asked.

"What?"

"A bath." She chuckled.

"I know something better." He picked up the candle, padded across the room back to the linen closet and extracted a couple of towels and bathrobes from the shelves. When he returned he set them on the table.

"What are you up to?" Her tittering was so charming it mesmerized him. Deeper than he remembered, her voice sounded more mature, as was the woman before him.

"A shower." He grabbed her hand in his.

"No electricity means no hot water."

Her steps were hesitant as he led her to the sliding glass doors. It still rained, but it wasn't the torrential fall they had experienced when they arrived.

"Outside?" Her voice rose with surprise.

"Outside. It's nature's shower."

"You must be crazy." Her little girl giggle made him smile.

He led her out upon the deck. "Not crazy, just in love." His impulsive action had gifted them with a dark romantic setting. In the distance, lightning zigzagged across the sky, creating flashes which reflected off the billowing waves below.

The overhang blocked the rain, so he pulled her farther toward the railing. Cool, wet drops fell from above. He stretched his arms out wide and let the water and breeze wash over him. Several seconds passed before she stepped out and joined him.

Water beaded off her skin, following the curves of her body before gathering at her feet. Her hair was damp once again. She'd never looked so sexy.

What was it about a wet woman that made a man horny? His cock twitched. Damned if he wasn't ready to take her again.

"This is wonderful." She tipped her head to meet the rain and twirled around, laughing. "I haven't done this since I was a child." Another spin and she was back in his embrace. Her arms folded around his neck. She gazed up at him with longing in her eyes. "I never want to return to reality."

"You don't have to. Stay here—with me."

As if his words conjured the very uncertainty they were both attempting to avoid, the light in the kitchen flickered on. Electricity was restored.

She blinked away raindrops. "Nathan, it isn't that easy." She smoothed her palm over his cheek. "I have a life in Colorado, my practice, a house. I can't just walk away from it, and Mom lives with me." The ache in her voice squeezed his chest.

She wanted this as much as he, she had to.

"I know this is asking a lot of you, but transfer here." He gripped her hand in his, held it close to the shelter of his body. "We're always in need of doctors. When I spoke to Dr. Waters, he told me he was looking for someone at the hospital. Paige, we can make this work." A moment of uncomfortable silence followed, causing him to nervously continue. "I couldn't bear to lose you again." He wouldn't lose her again, even if he had to follow her to Colorado. "I love you. Say you'll stay."

She stared deep into his eyes, big tears filling hers—or were they raindrops? "I want to say yes." A weak smile appeared. "I want to throw caution to the wind and say yes, but—"

"No buts. Say yes." His heart fluttered with hope.

She licked her lips and blinked. "Yes."

Joy like he'd never felt before overtook him. He wrapped his arms around her waist and raised her off her feet, turning in circles.

She laughed, hugging his neck.

When he lowered her, his lips found hers. She tasted of hope and a future together. Hand in hand, they ran back into the house dripping wet. He jerked a robe off the table and held it open, and she shoved her arms through it. He tightened her sash before slipping into a robe himself. As he closed the sliding glass doors, he tossed her a towel. She rapidly wiped the cloth over her legs and then ran it over her head to dry her hair. He did the same.

"If you want to take a quick shower, I'll fix us something to eat," he offered. Sylvia had never liked to cook, so he had gotten used to fixing meals for Cami and Janis.

Paige followed him into the kitchen. "No. I want to help."

Slender arms wrapped around his waist and he smiled. This was just how he'd imagined it would be between the two of them, working together, a real family. "Great." He turned in her embrace and looked into misty eyes. "Happy?"

She blinked back tears. "Ecstatic." Her arms locked around his neck. "Now kiss me."

As her lips touched his, he knew their life together had just begun.

Chapter Eight

Fate sure had a way of making itself known. Who would have guessed that deviating from her travel plans would land Paige right into the arms of the man she longed for? The god of fate deserved a huge thank you.

Shrugging out of her robe, she placed it atop the bed, before reaching into the bag and extracting a silky piece of material. Ebony black with red hibiscus and yellow centers accentuated by deep green leaves, the cloth slid through her fingertips as she draped it around her neck and then crisscrossed it over each breast.

"Now if I can only remember how the salesclerk said to fasten it." Reaching behind her, she struggled to connect the clasp. On the second try she was successful.

Next she stepped into the skirt that rode her hips like it was caressing them. The wide split up the front emphasized her long legs, while the back of the sarong stroked midway down her calves. Three-inch dress sandals would give her just the look she was searching for, sensual and feminine. Tonight she would go commando to avoid panty lines since the material hugged her like a second skin. Besides, it would be something to tease Nathan with throughout the evening.

A soft smile touched her lips at the wanton temptress staring back at her in the mirror. She ran her hands down her body and a delicious tremor assailed her. "This works," she whispered.

As she was placing a couple things in her black clutch purse, Nathan entered the bedroom and came to an abrupt halt. Wide-eyed and slack-jawed, he ogled her.

Pride and female satisfaction beamed through her like a light.

It took a moment for him to speak. When he did, his voice thickened. "You're gorgeous, baby." With just a few steps he closed the distance between them. Heavy-lidded, he raised a hand and smoothed a fingertip down her silk-covered breast, teasing a nipple.

Tingles erupted at the diamond-tips, zinging throughout her breasts, which were aching with need.

"I think we should stay right here." His hungry stare was pinned on her chest. Heat sizzled across her body, nearly stealing her breath. Moisture built between her naked thighs, making them wet and slick.

How the hell did he do that with just a look?

She managed a taut chuckle. "No way. You promised me a night out." Besides, she had plans for him later tonight. In fact, she might stoke his anticipation throughout the entire evening, starting now. She leaned in to rub against him.

He slowly raised his gaze to meet hers. "Then you have five seconds to get out of the bedroom before I strip you naked and have my way with you."

"Yeah. Right."

"One." His hand closed around one of her breasts. His thumb rubbed firmly over her nipple.

Oh Lord. He meant it. Her fingers tightened on her purse.

"Two."

"Okay. Okay. I'm going." She laughed, stepping backwards and pivoting. The click of her heels against the floor echoed as she hurried from the room.

Walking into the living room, Paige glanced out the window, and for the first time since she'd arrived in Kauai the gloomy weather didn't affect her. Sunshine sliced through the clouds, allowing a ray of light to shine upon the naupaka flower lying on the table next to Nathan's cell phone.

The sight of the flower filled her with excitement. "If that isn't a sign, I don't know what is."

She heard Nathan's footsteps behind her. "Who are you talking to?"

On the balls of her feet, she spun around. "No one. Just thinking out loud how lucky I am." She walked into his open arms.

In reality, Nathan was the lucky one. He had been given a second chance and this time he wouldn't screw it up. Her uncertainty was easy to understand and that was why he had to work double time to win her trust. "We better get going."

She eased up against him. "Where are you taking me?"

Her cherry-red lips called to him. He licked along the seam, nipping her bottom lip. "You'll see." She grinned, flicking her tongue against his before retreating. "Teasing me?" His voice deepened as his cock firmed against her belly.

"No. Just starting the evening off right with you hard and wanting me." Her velvet-smooth voice awoke all his senses. She stepped out of his embrace, took several steps, and then shot a sensual glance over her shoulder. "By the way, I'm not wearing any panties."

Nathan nearly swallowed his tongue. From a scale of one to

ten, his erection went from a four to ten within a single heartbeat. Weak-kneed, he stood there until he could catch his breath. "You're kidding, right?"

She turned back around. His gaze glued to her swaying hips as she approached. Looking up at him with a mischievous grin, she took his hand and placed it on her ass. "Would I lie to you?"

He ran his palm across her gentle swell. Red-hot need slammed into his balls, making his toes curl. Sure enough, she was naked beneath. He licked his suddenly dry lips. "Uh, baby, let's just stay here." So damn aroused, he doubted he could make it out to the Hummer much less through the evening without touching her. Her hands smoothed from his shoulders to his chest and lower, stopping just above his throbbing organ. He groaned when she snatched her hand away.

"Let's not. See ya in the car." She winked and slipped out the door.

He took a moment to adjust himself, and then, gingerly, he traced her steps.

When he approached the Hummer, Paige was already seated in the passenger seat. A cool breeze whipped around him. He opened the car door and slid inside.

No panties kept whispering through his mind.

The sly smile she gifted him was nothing compared to the slow teasing way she inched her knees apart.

His heart fluttered. His erection jerked.

Oh she was good.

Mesmerized by the woman, he'd completely forgotten his keys were still in his pants. He raised his hips and dug into his pocket. When her tongue slid seductively between her lips, he thought he'd died and gone to heaven. He would give his left nut to have that precious mouth wrapped around his aching shaft right here—right now.

He lowered his ass back upon the seat, before he crammed the key into the ignition and gave it a twist. As he steered the car for the road, her perfectly groomed fingernails slid up her legs.

Damn. That was sexy. He could almost swear he felt her fingernails trailing up his legs, knees and thighs, getting closer to the area that throbbed with need.

"Mmmm." She continued to stroke and smooth her hands along her bare limbs to the point he had to remind himself to breathe. "Feels. So. Good." Dark and sensuous, her voice sent a tremor through him.

That voice. It was almost as incredible as her stimulating touch.

He attempted to focus on the road, but found it impossible. She released a sexy groan that made him jerk the steering wheel when he looked her way.

"Sonofabitch." He righted the car before palming himself through his pants.

One of her hands had disappeared beneath her skirt. He couldn't see exactly what she was doing, but his imagination soared with the possibilities.

Did her expression of ecstasy mean she had parted her slit and was finger-fucking herself? The thought of her hand moving in and out of her hot sex made him impossibly harder. Or was she teasing the bundle of nerves nestled at the apex of her thighs?

"Talk to me, baby." He wanted to know every little dirty detail.

"Wet. Slick." Her body seemed to melt in the seat. Her

eyelids fell as she spread her knees wider and slouched down. She moved her hand back and forth, an expression of pure rapture spread across her face.

His grip on the wheel tightened. "Open your eyes," he growled. "Look at me."

She did as he demanded. Her smoky eyes were laden with lust. "Nathan. I need you inside me."

And that's exactly where he wanted to be, thrusting between her thighs.

He didn't think twice as he jerked the vehicle over to the side of the road. Her purse slid off the dashboard to the floor. "You know we might get caught?" Hell. They were on the highway. It was a certainty they would be discovered.

"I don't care. I ache for you." The hard edge in her voice thrilled him.

For a mere instant, the thought of them locked in jail for indecent exposure passed through his mind. Then again, a man would be an idiot to let an opportunity like this pass by—and Nathan Cross was no idiot.

He left the engine running and opened his door at the same time she did. They met before the hood of the vehicle and fell into each other's arms. He wasted no time pushing down his pants, before looping his arms beneath her knees to raise her against the vehicle and spread her wide.

Paige murmured her approval, crossing her mouth over his. Her hunger was overwhelming. She kissed him like a woman starving for a man's touch.

The second he thrust deep inside her, she cried out and he swallowed the sound. He couldn't remember when he had ever felt her so wet, so tight, so fucking wild as she moved hard and fast against him.

She grabbed his ass, held him closer.

A punch of excitement hit him in the belly and his knees went weak. Prickles of sensation raced across his skin as he drove her against the vehicle. His hips moved rapidly, pounding ferociously between her thighs. His climax hung on by a thread. If she pulled the string, he would completely come unraveled.

Her fingernails bit into his flesh, the sting bittersweet. "Oh God!" She shuddered, her back arching.

His hips churned against hers. "Not now. Wait." A burn radiated through his cock so hot that he struggled to hold on, make it last forever. He needed to savor the pleasure/pain, wanted her to feel what he did, because if he didn't know better he was coming apart in her arms.

Shaking, her body covered in a light mist of perspiration, she gasped. "Can't. Oh God."

Her swollen pussy sucked him deeper. Spasms rippled around him, setting off a fire that sizzled through his veins. He fought to breathe, fought to resist the claws of his orgasm demanding release.

But it was too late.

Nathan stiffened. The slow-motion eruption confused his dazed mind. He thought he heard Paige scream his name as every nerve ending began to beat with a pulse of its own. The rapture inside him built like an ocean's swell. He felt the wave's gravitational pull taking him higher and higher. The crest hung over him and then burst, raining pleasure and tossing him into the flames of ecstasy. It burned—it felt so good that for a moment he heard nothing.

Then Paige's frantic voice cut through his tattered mind. "Truck!" she cried out. "Let me down. Let me down."

Once again, it was too late.

As her feet touched the ground the large delivery truck's horn bellowed. The high-pitched sound seemed to go on forever, even when it raced around the curve and was out of sight.

A sheepish grin fell across Nathan's face. Damn. He hoped he didn't know the driver. Before anyone else caught them, he stuffed his dick back in his pants and fastened them.

Paige swayed. She fought to get her land legs beneath her. "I can't believe this." Her voice shook with laughter. "I'll have the reputation as a slut before I leave this island."

He chuckled, moving around the vehicle to open her door. "Not a slut, but perhaps a temptress."

"Not funny." She slapped him playfully on the shoulder, before she slid inside.

He leaned down and kissed her softly. "That was so fucking hot. Do you have any idea what you do to me?"

Her face beamed. "No, but if it's anything like what you do to me then I can imagine it."

He pressed his lips to hers once more. "I think you made us late." He slammed the door shut and hurried around to climb in behind the wheel.

When his door closed, she faced him. "Me?" She said it so innocently all he could do was laugh.

He shifted the Hummer into gear and pulled onto the road. "Yes. You were the one masturbating in the front seat of my car."

The prettiest pink dotted her cheeks. "Okay. I guess if you put it that way, perhaps I was to blame."

"Did you enjoy it?"

The color on her face deepened.

"Truth," he pressured.

"Yes. There, I said it. I enjoyed the hell out of it."

Rather pleased with himself, Nathan's lips quirked into a smile. "I've decided you should never wear panties again."

Her brows rose. "You have?"

As he maneuvered the vehicle off the highway he grinned. "In fact, I think I'll keep you naked and chained to my bed."

She giggled, the sound so carefree. "You might have to. We're not safe outside the bedroom. We always get caught."

"Admit it," he said. "Admit that you enjoy the daring, the possibility of having an audience. Tell me it doesn't make your body writhe knowing someone is watching. Confess that you're hot and bothered, maybe even a little wet and aroused."

"Yes, I'm aroused." She glanced around at the estate and the grounds surrounding it. "Where are we?"

"Home, Paige."

Chapter Nine

"Home?" An uneasy feeling slithered up Paige's back. Nathan pulled the Hummer before a majestic wrought-iron gate. He pushed a button on his dashboard, and the portal moaned as it slid open.

A smile twitched at the corners of his mouth. "I want you in my bed tonight." He squeezed her leg before he placed his hand back on the steering wheel and drove through the entrance on a cobblestone driveway. "I've dreamed about bringing you here for the past five years. I think you'll like it. I designed it myself."

Electric torches and tall palm trees lined the driveway leading to the large two-story estate that took Paige's breath away.

Instead of parking in the four-car garage, he pulled alongside the front of the house and switched off the engine. Paige didn't stir as he opened his door and moved quickly around the car to let her out.

"Everything okay?" he asked.

She gazed up at him. "This is your home?"

He extended his hand to her. "Our home."

Wide-eyed, she scanned what had to be at least ten acres of neatly groomed grounds with palm trees and a host of others, including lush tropical plants. "It's so beautiful and big."

Paige had never expected such extravagance.

He nestled his hand in the small of her back and guided her toward the door. "I love it here. I would have lost the house in the divorce if it hadn't been a part of my parents' estate. They had foreseen the disastrous outcome of our marriage long before I had admitted it."

"Who lives over there?" Paige pointed to a host of lights off to the west.

"That's the servants' cottage."

"Servants?" she repeated. Nathan had servants?

Paige had always been a little uncomfortable with his family's wealth. Hell. She came from simple roots, a single-income home. She would never be used to this type of extravagance.

"Housekeeper, landscaper and chef."

"Oh my." She released a heavy sigh, unable to wrap her mind around the grandeur of the place.

"Courtesy of the resort. You'll have whatever you want at your fingertips."

An awkward silence lingered between them.

He dipped a finger beneath her chin and raised her gaze to meet his. "You okay?"

"It's just a little overwhelming." She licked her lips. "I'm a simple woman. It's not exactly what we had planned." She felt wretched the moment the words left her mouth. "I'm sorry. I didn't mean—"

"Don't be sorry." He pressed a soft kiss upon her nose. "Our dreams were smaller in scale. Things are different now."

That was an understatement.

Before he opened the door he turned to her. "Truth is I built this home with you in mind. Yes, it got a little grander
114

with Sylvia's demands and needs."

Paige's body went rigid with the mention of his ex's name. She didn't want to think of this home as another woman's.

"Dammit. I'm sorry. We could move if you prefer, but I would like to stay here. This has been Cami's home since she was born."

"Of course." Paige inhaled deeply. "I just never expected such lavish accommodations."

"That's why I love you so much." Excitement glowed in his eyes. He grabbed her hand and squeezed. "Let me show you around."

On each side of the double oak doors stood a huge bird of paradise, which looked like sentries guarding the entrance. Over two dozen orange and blue flowers protruded from green spathes, each resembling a bird in flight.

Keys jiggled as he extracted them and opened the door. She stepped inside and her breath caught. It wasn't that she had never been in such a beautiful home, it's that it would be hers someday and the thought overwhelmed her.

"The main residence is comprised of koa and swamp mahogany wood milled right from the property. Come here, I want to show you something." He led her toward the large stone fireplace and the beautiful mantelpiece above it. As they approached, he turned on another light so that it flooded the room. "You have to bend low, but it's legible."

She leaned down, looking beneath the shelf where he pointed, and saw their initials carved in the wood. Tears touched her eyes. "You cut the tree down?" She reflected back to the large koa tree in front of the cottage that she'd noticed was gone when she arrived. "I can't believe you did this." Her finger traced the heart that embraced their display of love that summer and the month that followed before their engagement.

"You did love me."

"Do, baby." He took her into his arms. "You can add *always will* to that."

"I missed you so much," she choked back.

"I'm sorry, Paige. I did what I felt was right."

"I know, but knowing that didn't make it hurt any less."

"I did it for Cami. She means the world to me."

"I know and that's what makes me love you and honestly scares me."

He loosened his hold on her. "Scares you?"

The muscles in her throat tightened. "Will I be tossed aside again if Cami doesn't accept me?"

"Look at the way she interacted with you at the hospital. It's only a matter of time before she adores you. It might not be easy in the beginning, but she'll come around."

"But what if she doesn't?"

"Trust me, Paige." He sounded so confident.

If only she felt the same.

Nathan laid his warm cheek beneath her palm as they stood before the mantel he had etched their love into. A symbol that he had cherished what they had so long ago. The show of affection didn't erase her insecurities, didn't stop the frantic beating of her heart at the thought of her waking up one morning to find all the promises he'd made her over the last couple days had disappeared.

She wasn't ready to let him go, but she heard herself say, "We haven't really considered Cami's needs. The experts recommend a year before you start to date or introduce a new individual within a child's life after a divorce."

"No." He pulled Paige so close she could feel his heated breath across her face. His intense glare made her pause. "I'm not letting you go. Don't ask that of me. I want you here with us, now."

The voice of reason rang in her ears. "Nathan, divorce is a stressful time for everyone involved, particularly for the children." How many times had she seen this scenario in the troubled children who had come to her office? "Children lose their sense of home, family and belonging. They can act up and become physically ill. It's like mourning the death of a loved one."

Something she said must have struck a nerve because he became nonplused. The intensity in his features changed to one of concern. It nearly killed her to continue.

"Not to mention, children always manage to convince themselves that they contributed to divorce. It's their fault Mommy and Daddy aren't together anymore." To make things worse, when either of the parents finally decided to move on and start dating, they often do so with less regard for the children. Nathan loved Paige, but maybe he wasn't thinking clearly about the situation. "Dating after divorce should be put off until the child has had time enough to heal." Each word cut through her heart like a knife. This was exactly what her mother had been warning her against. If only Paige had used her head and not her heart.

He blew out a silent breath. His Adam's apple slid up and down like he had something caught in his throat. "It's not like that with you and me," he said softly. "I never loved Sylvia like I do you. There is no bond—no chemistry like there is with us."

"But—"

His hands buried in her hair as he covered her mouth with his. The kiss lacked any semblance of tenderness. His hands were hard, dominant, making sure she didn't move. He devoured her as if he hungered for something that wasn't his. The harsh sounds that tore from his throat were heartbreaking.

When the caress ended she tried to catch her breath, but her raging emotions made it hard to inhale. It didn't help when Nathan pressed his cheek to hers, his voice steady and low. "You're mine, Paige. You always have been. You always will be." He released her. "Now if we're through with this conversation, there's more for you to see."

Paige had never seen this dominant side of Nathan. His heavy steps screamed his determination. She caught up with him as he reached the kitchen. "You can't just ignore that a problem exists."

He hesitated, before inhaling deeply. "I'm not a fool, Paige." His voice was eerily low. "Is it going to be easy? There's only one question all this hinges on."

Question?

"Do you love me?" His tone softened and she melted inside.

She blinked back tears, nodding. "With all my heart."

"Then everything else will work out." He cupped her cheeks. "Okay?"

"Okay," she muttered. Emotion thickened in her belly.

"Now, are you hungry?"

"Hungry?" Bewildered, she cast her gaze around the room. They stood in the dining room, soft candlelight flickering, the long mahogany table set for two. "No. Show me the rest of the house first."

They moved from one room to the next. One thing was consistent—the highest quality furniture, fixtures and accessories decorated each room. As well as pictures, lots of photographs of Sylvia, Nathan and Cami adorned the walls and the knickknack shelves, including the large mantel with their initials.

"You can change anything you like. I'm not opposed to modifying anything except this room." He pushed the double doors wide and revealed a bedroom worth dying for.

The large mahogany bed had bedposts that were at least eight feet tall. From their peaks black wrought iron arched and curved to meet in the middle. The head and footboards were massive. The décor was definitely a male's choice with the exception of the intricate roses and leaves carved into the rich wood. There were two matching dressers with mirrors, an ornate armoire, and a wall unit that housed a large television set. One wall of the room was nothing but glass.

Nathan strolled to the window and something clicked. With a push he slid the panels along the tracks that ran across the floor. The salty ocean breeze and the sweet scent of flowers filled the room. He stepped out on the veranda and looked into the darkened sky where a handful of stars shone through. The promise of rain hung heavy.

It should have been the most romantic setting Paige had ever been in. Instead, all she could think about was Sylvia and Nathan making love in that big four-poster bed. Her stomach churned with jealousy as she clutched her purse to her breasts. She knew it was childish, but she didn't want to sleep in the same bed that his ex had occupied.

He must have recognized her uneasiness, because he said, "Come here." When she was near enough to touch, he snaked his arms around her waist and drew her close. "Sylvia never slept in this bed. I had the room redesigned when she moved out."

The breath she hadn't known she'd held rushed out of her lungs in relief.

He held her against him and for a moment they let the world revolve around them. No one existed but the two of them. No lingering issues hung around their necks like a noose.

The warmth of his hand smoothed downward and stopped in the small of her back. "Let me show you the master bathroom." They moved back into the bedroom, and he slid the glass shut. She set her purse on the big, inviting bed before following him through a large arched entry.

She gasped in awe. "I've never seen anything so luxurious." White marble with reddish-brown veins throughout covered the floor, walls, countertops, shower and sunken tub. Chocolate brown sheers held back by velveteen ties framed the window. Like the bedroom, the panels were on tracks which opened up to a deck containing two lounge chairs, a small table and a Jacuzzi. Foamy bubbles extended an invitation to test the waters.

"There's a wall of foliage around this area, providing privacy. You can sunbathe nude or relax in the Jacuzzi without fear of voyeurs." He paused before adding, "Of course, that's never stopped us before." His playful grin made her chuckle. "Should we try it out?" He opened the glass, stepped out into the night and turned to extend a hand to her. "Join me."

Why did she fight the rollercoaster of emotions she felt every time he looked at her with those penetrating eyes? All her common sense seemed to take flight. She walked into his arms.

He held her for a moment. "I want you." His avowal hummed in her ear. When he released her, he stepped behind her so she faced the foliage. The building breeze tugged at her clothing and tossed her hair about as it rustled the leaves and plucked at the flowers adorning them.

Deft fingers unfastened the halter top that hung around her neck and crisscrossed in the front. The material parted into two pieces and drifted between her bare breasts, but not before rasping softly against her sensitive nipples. Add the cool wind and a shudder assailed her. Anticipation of his touch made the peaks draw into tight buds. "Nathan."

"Shush, baby. Close your eyes." His words released a flood of moisture between her thighs. He brushed aside her hair and kissed her bare shoulder, sending chills across her arms.

A gentle pull at her skirt and her eyelids fell. Her waistband loosened, followed by the achingly slow whisper of the garment's zipper. Heat raced across her body as her arousal climbed. She couldn't wait for him to strip her bare, bend her over the Jacuzzi, spread her wide and take her hard and fast, or maybe slow and tender. The image of his hands all over her body, the feel of his mouth against hers and his cock thrusting inside her, made the throb between her legs thicken.

"Do you know how beautiful you are?" His voice slid across her skin, the sensation as sensual as the silky skirt caressing her legs on its descent.

In seconds she was naked with nothing on but her black, three-inch heels. Even though Nathan and Paige were hidden by all eyes, just the thought of being unclothed outside with him standing behind her sent her senses reeling.

"Are your eyes closed?" His breath was warm against her neck.

She swallowed hard. "Yes."

"Good." He rested his palms on her hips. "I want to touch you until you scream for me to take you." To make his point he pressed his engorged erection firmly against her ass.

Thunder bellowed, a powerful, reverberating sound that came one after another to raise her anxiety. Every once in awhile a flash of light penetrated her eyelids.

"I want you now." Her admission came without shame. She needed him naked and pounding between her thighs with the ferocity of the approaching storm. The scent of rain blended with Nathan's earthy cologne, thrilling her. Yet it couldn't compare to the strong hands that smoothed over her hips, down her abdomen to cup the small patch of hair below.

Her inner muscles clenched tight and a wave of desire lashed throughout. On a gasp, her lips parted. "Now, Nathan. Take me now." With a single finger he applied pressure to her clit and she groaned. "Please."

"Spread your legs."

Paige thought it would be easy to follow his demand, but as she inched her feet apart her pussy spasmed. The need to pinch her thighs together was strong, but she prevailed, moving her legs shoulder-width apart. His wicked fingertips reached between their bodies and caressed her swollen folds for just a second before his hand retreated, only to return. On the third—or was it the fourth?—swipe, he flicked her clit, sending a ray of pleasure quaking though her core.

"Now," she cried out. "Nathan, fuck me now."

"So wet. Are you tight?" He didn't wait for an answer. He shoved a finger deep inside her.

Her knees threatened to buckle. She felt dizzy as her sex tightened and released, over and over.

"Oh yeah. I can feel you sucking on my finger." His seductive tone was nearly her undoing. "I can't wait until your body is sucking on my cock."

Her need soared. "Damn you, Nathan."

The next release of thunder felt like it vibrated through her womb. As he pumped his finger in and out, she didn't know how much longer she could hold on. She cupped her own breasts, fingers finding the taut nipples, and squeezed. A whirling mass of sensations burst through her swollen flesh and shot south to intensify the spasms.

"That's it, baby, touch yourself." His voice deepened. "Pinch them hard."

She did and groaned with the pleasure/pain washing through her.

His finger vanished from her body and she whimpered. "Please don't do this to me."

Quick little kisses whispered down the small of her back. His large hand cupped her ass, parting her cheeks. She trembled. When his warm, wet tongue trailed a seductive path between the cleft of her ass, she almost lost it. Her heart jolted like it would jump out of her chest. She gasped as he swirled his tongue near her anus. Every muscle throughout her body grew taut, and her fingers on her breasts stilled.

Stars burst behind her eyelids. "Nathan!"

"Hold on, baby."

Nathan released Paige and moved quickly around her. He fell to his knees and gazed up. Her head was thrown back, her hands gripping her breasts. The sight of her nipples between her fingers and thumbs made his balls throb with the need to fuck her and to do it now, but first he had to taste her.

Spreading her thighs wider, he settled between them. Her musk was an aphrodisiac calling to him. He dipped his head and circled his tongue over her swollen clit. She bucked against him and screamed his name for a second time. She trembled as he parted her juicy slit and lowered his head.

The taste of her exploded against his taste buds. Sweet. Tart. A mixture of heaven.

"Mine," he murmured against her heated skin.

"Oh God." She grabbed his shoulders, fingernails biting into his flesh. A low groan eased from her lips as her climax erupted and liquid fire burst upon his tongue. Her body convulsed around him.

A growl rumbled in his throat.

He drank greedily at her pussy until his khakis felt too tight. His cock strained against the zipper, demanding freedom, and still he devoured her. He loved the way she writhed against him. With each contraction her body pulled him deeper and deeper.

When he looked up, she stared down at him with the most sated expression. Her chest rose and fell rapidly. Her hands drifted to her sides. He pushed to his feet. Neither spoke as he tore his shirt over his head and flung it aside. She looked like a siren, naked in only her black stilettos. The wind blew her hair around her face and shoulders. Her pussy was slick, swollen and pink, urging him to take her.

He kicked out of his shoes and reached for the waistband of his pants. When they were unfastened, he pushed them down his legs and stepped out.

Lust reflected back at him when he looked deep into her eyes. Without a word, he grabbed her hand and led her to the small table. "Bend over."

She did as he requested without hesitation. In the dim light he stared at her heels, his hungry gaze traveling up her long legs to the gentle swells of her ass. She glanced back at him. The image of her legs parted, bent over and waiting for him to fuck her, took his breath away. His chest grew tight.

"God, you're sexy."

As if to confirm the effect she had on him, his dick screamed in pain, begging to push inside her. He moved behind her and pressed the head of his erection against the moist entrance of her sex. Arching his hips, he watched as the swollen, naked lips of her pussy parted, inviting him in. He pulled back and pressed forward again. Oh yeah. He loved the way her body welcomed him as he worked his cock into her a little deeper.

Heat sizzled from the small slit of the sensitive head and down his shaft. With each thrust her tight body pulled and released his foreskin to slide against the ridged bands on the underside of his erection. A taut breath eased through clenched teeth. "Feels so good." He threw his head back and pushed the last inches in, hips flush against her ass. When the suction of her body clamped down on him, he withdrew and plunged forward, again and again.

"Fuck." His sensitive balls slapped her ass, the sound so erotic they throbbed with a vengeance. His cock lengthened almost to the point of pain.

And then she moaned. Her inner muscles clenched and flexed harder, faster, to send him careening into a frenzy of pleasure.

"God yes," he hissed.

Thunder cracked and his release exploded, almost blinding him as it ripped from his scrotum and burned down his cock. All-consuming love for Paige wrapped around him. The connection he felt was as if his very soul was ripped from him and flowed into her. Collapsing against her back, he struggled to breathe. If he hadn't been leaning against her, he might have fallen.

Cool, wet raindrops sprinkled on his back. They fell easy at first. Suddenly, a sonic boom of thunder tore open the sky and a torrent came down. Nathan and Paige startled, parting. As she ducked her head and ran for the safety of the bathroom, he gathered their clothing and his shoes, following her inside.

"That was a surprise ending to wonderful sex." She laughed, shaking her head to send drops of water everywhere.

He spread their clothing on the countertop and towel racks, before he walked to the shower and turned on the faucets. "Want to join me?"

She kicked off her heels. "Sure."

Lukewarm water rained over them as they stepped beneath the two-headed spigots. After several pumps of the liquid soap container attached to the wall, he placed his hands on her shoulders and began to cleanse her body.

"Mmmm." She tilted her head to one side. "That feels good."

His palms glided across her like silk until she was covered head-to-toes in suds.

She turned in his arms, pressing her body to his. "Now it's my turn." Instead of retrieving soap from the container, she slowly rubbed her chest over his. The hard peaks of her nipples whispered over his chest, making his cock twitch.

Looking deep into her eyes, he smoothed his palms down her arms and smiled. "I'd almost forgotten what a talent you had in the shower."

She softly laughed, turning her back to him. With long, slow caresses, she slid her ass against his firming erection.

The ringing of a telephone cut through the heat building in his groin. He raised his head and listened. "I probably should get that." No one usually called after nine and it was nine thirty. Cami would be in bed by eight, so it probably had something to do with the resort. Paige faced him, and he planted a quick kiss on her lips. He rinsed off and stepped from the shower, grabbing a towel off the rack to dry off, before he secured it around his waist. Padding across the room, he headed toward the telephone on the nightstand. The minute he was within reach the phone quit ringing. The caller ID revealed it was his mother. His fingers curled around the receiver, stopping midway when Paige entered the room.

Damn. She was beautiful.

He released the telephone. If it had been important, his mom would have called him on his cell phone. As he approached Paige, he made a mental note to call his mother in the morning.

"Dinner, dessert or another round between the sheets?" he asked. "I think I ordered a Hawaiian chocolate cake."

"Cake or you?" She pinched her lips together. "Hmmm. That's a hard choice." She eased against him. "I choose you."

He pulled the towel from around his hips and tossed it aside. He would never get enough of her.

"I've missed you so much." She paused before wrapping her arms around his neck and pulling him to her. Just before their lips touched, she breathed, "Love me, Nathan, like you'll never let me go."

"What about dinner?"

"We'll eat it for breakfast," she said.

Slanting his mouth over hers, he caught her weak mewl. Her embrace tightened and she hardened the caress. Her lips moved over his with a need that was soul deep, before their mouths parted on a ragged breath.

Her head lolled back on a gasp and he took the moment to shower her neck with light kisses. His cock pressed hard against her belly as he grabbed her around the waist and raised her off the floor. He couldn't wait to get her in his bed where she belonged.

With shuffled steps he headed toward the bed. The storm continued to rage outside. Rain pounded against the window as if demanding entrance. Gently he placed her upon the comforter and then took several steps backward.

His erection lengthened at the sight of her. Naked, her lips kiss swollen, she looked at him through feathered lashes. Red-hot desire flared with each shift of her body as she eased back, propping herself on a pillow. She raised her hips and jerked the forest green comforter from beneath her, tossing her purse to the floor. She softly patted the place beside her.

He kneeled on the mattress, and it moaned beneath his weight.

Her lips curved into a sexy grin as she inched her thighs apart.

Soft. Pink. Moist, swollen folds called to him. He crawled toward her and eased between her legs. His throbbing cock pressed against her entrance as he lowered his chest, sealing their bodies together. He was about to close the distance between their lips when he heard footsteps. The doorknob twisted.

"Daddy?" Cami's voice made his eyes spring wide.

"Oh God," he whispered. "What is she doing home?" A feeling of dread swept over him. The door was unlocked. Adrenaline rushed through his veins, making his heart pound faster. Cami couldn't find him and Paige like this. With quick, jerky movements he rolled off her. As the door flew open, he and Paige reached for the sheet at the same time. Their struggle left them both half exposed when the door opened.

"Daddy, I'm home—" The sweetness in Cami's voice faded as her eyes widened in surprise. The smile on her face crumbled. "Daddy?" Her bottom lip started to quiver.

"Hey, sweetheart." His voice cracked. How the hell was he going to explain Dr. Weston in his bed? "I didn't expect you home."

"Obviously." The snide comment was female and definitely familiar. When Sylvia stepped through the doorway, Nathan felt his ex's presence like a blow to the stomach.

This couldn't be good.

Chapter Ten

Oh. My. God.

Lying next to Nathan, Paige couldn't believe the nightmare unfolding before her. His daughter and ex-wife stared at them as if they had committed adultery. Even though he was divorced, the heat of shame swept across her cheeks. She tightened her knuckles around the sheet stretched between them and looked into Sylvia's eyes, which were filled with resentment. Cami's silent tears were difficult to confront. The contempt on her mother's face wasn't much better, until her expression melted into one of sorrow and pain.

"How could you do this to our child?" Sylvia pulled Cami into the shelter of her tall, slender frame. "I can't believe that you would introduce a woman into our daughter's life s-so soon, especially *that* woman." Her bitterness bled through her now-flowing tears. "I can't stay here now. I'm leaving."

Cami gasped, jerking her startled gaze to her mother's. Grasping at Sylvia's short skirt, the little girl burst into hysterics. "Mommy, no. Daddy, tell her to stay. Tell her you want her here."

Nathan glanced at Paige. Her heart raced. What would he say?

He ran his fingers through his hair. "I'm sorry." The tears in his eyes were killing her.

Sorry? Paige's mind whirled. Sorry, that this was happening? Or sorry that he once again would walk out on her? The air in the room thickened. She couldn't breathe.

"Baby, I need the sheet." While he rose, securing the linen around his waist, Paige used the comforter to cover herself. When he reached Cami, he knelt so that his gaze met hers. "Remember your mother doesn't live here anymore."

Paige almost gagged on the relief she inhaled.

"She came back." Cami released her mother's leg. "Mommy said she'd stay if you wanted her to." The child choked back sobs that made Paige's chest ache. From the agony furrowing Nathan's brow, his daughter's sadness was breaking his heart too.

He blinked away moisture as he reached for Cami. "Honey, listen to me." When she jerked away, burying her face back into her mother's leg, he looked at Paige as if saying, "I don't know what to do." The anguish in his eyes was gut-wrenching. "Cami. Please." His voice shook. "We talked about this. Your mother lives in New York now."

"No!" Cami stomped her foot, refusing to face him. "She wants to come home." Suddenly, she spun around and flew into her father's embrace. Her little arms circled his neck. "Please, Daddy. Please let Mommy come home."

"Janis," he yelled over his daughter's shoulder. "Baby." His voice cracked again as his tone softened. "You know that isn't possible." When Cami didn't hear what she wanted, her arms and legs flailed. She fought against her father's hold. Her cries rose to a heartbreaking pitch. He held her close, burying his face into her shoulder. "Please understand."

A tear rolled down Paige's cheek. Cami was too young to understand grown-up games, and Paige had no doubt in her mind that this was a game. Even as Sylvia wiped at her alligator tears, Paige could see the smile within. She had no sympathy for a parent who used their child to manipulate their ex-spouse. In fact, it made her madder than hell.

Did Nathan realize Sylvia's ploy?

When Janis came into the room, she glanced at Paige lying in the bed. Her eyes widened. "Oh my God," she whispered before pinning her gaze on Nathan. "I'm so sorry. Sylvia said that she wanted to surprise—"

"Please take Cami upstairs." He raised his head, and Paige could see tears in his eyes. His child's pain was killing him.

"No. I don't want to go," Cami insisted, trying to hold on to him.

"Please, baby. Your mother and I need to talk." It wasn't his words that left a knot in Paige's throat, it was Sylvia's sudden smirk of triumph.

Nathan tried to hand Cami to Janis, but she jutted her arms out toward her mother. "Mommy." She tore herself from her father's embrace and ran to her mother.

"Come here, honey." Sylvia hugged her daughter, brushing the child's hair out of her eyes. "Go with Janis. I'll be up shortly." She kissed her on the forehead, and then she released Cami.

Janis picked the child up in her arms. "Did you see there are more presents beneath the Christmas tree? Let's count them before we go to your bedroom."

Before Cami left she turned her big blue eyes on Paige. "Get out of my house." The child's words were like a knife to her heart, slicing to the depths of her soul. Janis didn't hesitate, carrying the child out of the bedroom. Paige glanced at Sylvia. The woman's smile was all teeth and no warmth behind Nathan's back.

Releasing a heavy sigh, he pinched the bridge of his nose. "I need to get dressed." He sounded so forlorn. "Sylvia, wait for me in the living room."

"Of course." She headed toward the door as he disappeared into the bathroom.

Paige was about to throw back the covers when Sylvia drew to a stop and turned around. Daggers flashed in her eyes. "I hope you enjoyed my husband."

"Ex-husband," Paige reminded her.

Sylvia's soft laughter was pure evil. She stepped farther into the room. "Oh please. You must be a slow learner. Nathan will never be yours. Do you think he'll exchange Cami's happiness for yours or for that matter his?" She released a harrumph of disbelief to solidify her point. "This divorce means nothing."

Before Paige could respond, Nathan returned. He had donned only his wet khakis. Something close to disbelief filtered across his face, and then he frowned. "God, I should have known you wouldn't do what I asked." Barefoot, he crossed the room to the bed where Paige had inched into a sitting position. He dug deep into his pocket, extracting his keys. "Take the Hummer and go to the cottage. I'll take the Lexus in the garage and join you in a couple of hours." He dropped the keys into her palm. They felt cold against her trembling hand.

Heat flamed up her neck as she breathed in roughly and stared back at him. He was sending her away.

As if to rub her face into her insecurity, Sylvia raised a perfectly groomed eyebrow. "Don't wait up. He won't be leaving here."

Nathan spun around to face his ex-wife. "Shut up." His voice snapped like a whip.

Sylvia flinched, but she held her tongue.

He turned back to Paige. "I need to make sure Cami is okay. You do understand?"

Paige nodded. She could understand his need to ensure his daughter was well, but if they were to become a family as soon as Nathan had inferred, then she needed to be included. Instead she was the odd man out, again. She tried to tell herself that this wasn't a repeat of five years ago. That she would prevail this time. That Nathan loved her. That it couldn't be worse than what she had already endured. Yet strangely it felt the same. The ache in her chest was increasing with each ragged breath.

Paige pulled the comforter around her before she rose from the bed. She felt the coolness of the floor clear to her bones as she rushed into the bathroom. The door closed behind her and she clapped her hand over her mouth in an effort to hold back her cries. Numbing silence engulfed the room for long seconds, and then she heard Sylvia and Nathan start to argue.

After finding her clothes, she looped the top over her neck, made the crisscross over her breasts, but had a hell of a time securing the clasp because her hands were shaking so badly. The material was still damp, clinging to her body. She dragged her skirt up her legs, hips, and zipped it quickly as the voices beyond the door rose.

"What were you thinking?" she heard Nathan say.

"Nathan, please. Don't you see this is best for Cami? She needs us," Sylvia sobbed.

Nathan's silence was like a bullet to Paige's heart, which felt like it stopped beating at that moment. Air left her lungs in a single gush. "Don't listen to her. She's manipulating you." She choked on the plea clawing up her throat.

"You know I'm right," Sylvia added.

Nathan said something Paige couldn't hear. Did he agree

with his ex-wife? Was Paige losing him all over again?

Frantically, she began to look around for her shoes. After locating them, she slipped one heel on and then the other. Her legs felt wobbly, unable to hold her, but they did.

When she stepped into the bedroom, Nathan and Sylvia grew quiet. His ex's palm lay on his arm. The sight broke Paige's heart. His broad back shifted, muscles rippling beneath his skin. He turned toward her and the emptiness in his expression chilled her. Behind his back Sylvia's smug expression was enough to make Paige's stomach pitch. She'd seen that same look years ago. He walked toward her. She swallowed hard, preparing herself for the worst.

Paige trembled when his warm palms slid up her cold arms. "I'll see you soon." He kissed her softly on the lips.

The caress should have given her the reassurance she needed, but it didn't. Her chest rose and fell rapidly. She had to get out of there. Without saying goodbye, she spun around, spying her purse. She stopped to pick it up. When she rose, Sylvia had positioned herself by the door, her hand on the doorknob. She opened the door wide, allowing Paige to pass through it. On her way out, Sylvia whispered, "Don't wait up for him. Trust me. What Cami wants, Cami gets. She's like her mother."

The door slammed shut behind her and Paige jumped, feeling more than the door separating them. The sting of hot tears burned her eyes and for a moment she didn't move. When she did, she fled down the hall toward the exit. Her heels clicked against the floor. Her trembling fingers closed around the doorknob. She twisted and pushed at the same time, and the wind tore the door from her hands, nearly sucking her out of the house as if ejecting her. She fought to close the door, fought to restrain her emotion, but tears raced down her cheeks—or was it the rain falling from the sky?

Blurred vision hampered her steps as she made her way to the Hummer. She swiped at her eyes, but it did no good. Climbing inside the vehicle, all Paige could think of was that this couldn't be happening again.

No. She wouldn't believe the worst. He had kissed her, promised to come to her later tonight. With newfound determination, she stuck the key into the ignition and turned over the engine. She glanced into the rearview mirror. "Nathan loves me."

They could work through Cami's sadness.

They had to.

Nathan's chest felt tight. He rubbed his neck. All he could do was shake his head, remembering the shocked expression on Cami's face when she burst into the bedroom and found him with Paige. His daughter's tears had a way of ripping his heart out.

Sylvia approached him with a sway in her hips that he wasn't buying. There was no denying she was sexy and knew her way around a man's body, but the truth always bled through. Her beauty was only skin deep. The woman was selfish. She thought of no one but herself. Even their child took second to her needs and wants.

"Nathan, I know we've had our differences, but we can make this work." She placed her palm on his arm again and he cringed. He felt nothing for her but disgust. "For Cami's sake we can be a family again. Please, tell me you'll try."

He shrugged out of her grasp. "Why did you come back?"

"For Cami. You." She tried to touch him again, but he stepped out of her reach. "Us."

Her bottom lip quivered. It was cute on Cami, but manipulative on Sylvia. She used her sensuality to achieve her objectives. When that didn't work, she resorted to fake tears, like now. Her eyes welled with moisture, several drops squeezing from the corners.

"It's Christmas," she sobbed. "I couldn't bear being away from you. Cami." She said their daughter's name as if it were a second thought.

"How could you do this to Cami?" he asked. She had to have known how devastating it would be to their daughter finding him with Paige like this.

"Me? I had no idea that you'd have that whore in our bed."

The hackles on his neck rose at her demeaning words. "*My* bed, and Paige is more woman than you could ever be."

Fire flickered in her eyes, but she doused it almost as quickly as it appeared. "Nathan, please don't do this to us."

"We had our chance." Five years of fighting and bickering. There wasn't any room in his heart for more of the same, especially for Cami's sake. It wasn't healthy for a child to be around fighting parents all the time. It tore him up inside, but his daughter would have to understand. He couldn't live the life he had. Paige was the only woman he had ever wanted.

Sylvia huffed. Her backbone went rigid. "You never gave me or us a chance. That whore lay between us for the past five years."

Red-hot hatred for the woman standing before him raced up his neck. "I'm warning you, Sylvia."

"Can't you see it's fate, me showing up at this moment to stop you from making the biggest mistake of your life?"

"Fate? It's more like jealousy and a telephone call from Yolanda advising you that Paige was in town." He should have known the minute that woman left his sight at the mall she'd called his ex.

Sylvia tossed her long brunette hair over one shoulder. "Jealous of her?" Her brows pulled inward. "Please." As if realizing how she looked to him, her attitude changed swiftly. Her voice softened. "Don't you see, Nathan, she's like a poison in your veins. Why else would you toss our daughter's feelings aside for another?"

He wasn't tossing Cami's feelings aside. It's true that she hurt now. At four she was too young to understand the situation. Perhaps he should have treaded lightly. Maybe Paige was right about putting distance between them until Cami adjusted. Yet the thought of not holding Paige made him sick. His stomach churned.

"Send her away, Nathan." Sylvia moved closer, and he could smell her expensive perfume, a musky scent used to tantalize men. "Let's enjoy Christmas together, as a family. I've made all the arrangements. I've told your mother we wouldn't be joining them."

So that was why his mother had called him. She was trying to warn him that Sylvia was back. But why hadn't she called his cell phone? He briefly closed his eyes, remembering that he'd left his cell phone on the table in the cottage.

"I've called the resort and they will deliver dinner at three. Maybe you could whip us up some of your fabulous French toast for breakfast to hold us over." Excitement filled her voice. "I can't wait for you to see what I got you. Nathan." Her voice deepened, turned sexy as she gazed up at him through thick lashes. "We haven't christened this new bed." She sat upon the mattress that smelled of sex and Paige and gave a little bounce. "Let me love you tonight."

A knock on the bedroom door stole his attention, but not

before he saw Sylvia roll her eyes. He walked to the door and opened it.

From where Janis stood she had a straight shot to see Sylvia sitting on his bed. Her face reddened. "I'm sorry to bother you, but Cami is asking for you both."

"Can't you sing a song or read her a book? We're busy here," Sylvia barked.

"Um. Of course, I'm so sorry." Janis started to back away.

"Tell her we'll be in shortly." He closed the door and raised a brow as he turned to Sylvia.

"What?" She shrugged, raising her palms upward. "She'll be okay. Besides, it's time for her to be asleep."

He shook his head. "Then why did you get her up out of bed to take a boat ride on an unstable ocean in this weather?"

When would it dawn on Sylvia that it wasn't all about her?

She looked at him, her expression softening. "To be with you. I love you."

His laugh held no humor. Their conversation was leading nowhere. He cleared his throat. "Let me tell you how this is going down. Both of us will go upstairs to say good night to Cami. Then you'll tell her that you've made a mistake and that you're returning to New York tomorrow morning. You can stay in one of the guest bedrooms. In the morning we'll have breakfast and you can watch Cami open the presents that you brought for her. When she's finished, you'll say your goodbyes and then you'll get on the broom you came in on and leave."

Sylvia's jaw dropped.

Before she could respond, he continued. "This game is over. You can either help me make this easy on Cami or I swear I'll take you to court and fight for full custody. And believe me, Sylvia, I will win." He said the last three words with a confidence that made her mouth snap shut.

Both their families came from money. A court battle would be nasty and drawn out. His ace in the hole was that while he had been the doting father these past five years, Sylvia had not even attempted to cover her many indiscretions. He had a file of pictures and witnesses that he hadn't used on the first custody go-round because he believed Cami needed both her mother and father.

"Our daughter isn't a tool to be used at your beck and call. I won't let you hurt her. Either way, I'm marrying Paige."

"You fool." Sylvia spat the words. She sprang from the bed. Her eyes burned with resentment. "I'm not the one hurting Cami, you are." Anger reddened her face as she shook with fury. "If you think for a minute I'll allow that woman in my home, around my daughter, you're fucking crazy."

"My home. My daughter too," he said firmly.

He had never heard her growl, but the low, raspy sound bubbled up from her throat. She stomped by him and he grabbed her wrist. "Where the hell do you think you're going?"

She jerked her hand, but he held fast. "To get my daughter. We're out of here."

"Uh, no. I have court papers that say she's to be with me this holiday. Remember, it cost me a Ferrari." The damn woman had sold her time with her daughter for a car. He had never been so disgusted in his life. "Lay a single finger on that child and I'll have you arrested." In fact, he relished seeing the woman in handcuffs and behind bars. It would only make his case stronger.

She swung her free hand, but he caught it inches from his cheek.

"Bastard," she fumed. "Then you can explain to Cami why her mother isn't here in the morning or for that matter why you forced me to leave tonight without saying goodbye."

This time when she pulled away he let her go. Did her cruelty know no bounds? Would she really leave Cami without saying goodbye?

Before Sylvia made it to the door, she whipped around to face him. "Enjoy your life, Nathan, because I plan to make it a living hell." She jerked open the door and slammed it behind her.

The silence was bittersweet. Sylvia was gone, but now he had to face Cami.

Eleven o'clock shined in neon orange from the clock on his nightstand. He couldn't believe that it would soon be Christmas Eve and a shitty one at that. Maybe he should call Paige now. Let her know that he'd probably be late. Spearing his fingers through his hair, he knew he was avoiding the inevitable— facing Cami. He'd call Paige after he got Cami settled and asleep.

Each step felt leaden as he headed for the door. This was one confrontation he wasn't looking forward to. He just had to remember that children were incredibly resilient. With the right guidance he and Paige could work through this with Cami.

Chapter Eleven

Sitting with her feet tucked beneath her on the couch, Paige wrung her hands together. She raised her troubled gaze for the umpteenth time from the television to the cable box that sat on the shelf above. Eleven forty-five. It had been almost two hours since she had left Nathan's home. Each minute that slipped by added to her anxiety.

He isn't coming back, her subconscious cried.

"You're being ridiculous." Disgusted with her insecurity, she unfolded her legs and stood, tightening the sash around her waist. When she had arrived at the cottage she had stripped out of her wet clothes, opting for just the robe.

Outside the moon shone through the dark clouds, while the rain lightly fell. She knew this because she had opened the front door at least fifty times looking for Nathan.

"There are a number of things that could have detained him. Maybe the telephone lines are out." She walked back to the couch where the telephone sat on the coffee table and picked up the receiver. Her heart sank at the dial tone blaring in her ear. Slowly she placed the receiver back in its cradle. "That doesn't mean anything."

Do you really think that speaking aloud will change the outcome?

"Stop it." She stomped her bare foot like a child. "He

wouldn't do this to me again." She shored her shoulders. Even as she listened to her reassuring words, she wondered if she was fooling herself. Cami would always come first in Nathan's life. Paige didn't begrudge the child. She just wanted the opportunity to share him and to become part of their lives. She loved children. All she needed was a chance.

Once again, she paced to the front door, opened it and peered out. No headlights. No Nathan. The clean scent of the falling rain didn't soothe her like it usually did. Even the roar of the ocean went unnoticed.

Briiing. Briiing.

Paige almost jumped out of her skin. Not to mention, tripped over her feet as she slammed the door and ran toward the telephone. Breathless with anticipation, she raised the receiver to her ear. "Nathan?"

"Ahhh. You did wait up. How charming, but stupid." A sick sensation settled in the pit of Paige's belly at the sound of Sylvia's voice. "Honey, I'll take another glass of wine."

Oh my God. Paige clutched the receiver. Her heart stuttered. Was that Nathan's voice in the background? It was definitely male.

"Mmmm." The sexy moan Sylvia released made Paige's breath freeze in her lungs.

This couldn't be happening again.

Sylvia released a satisfied chuckle. "Like I said before, what Cami wants, Cami gets. Merry Christmas, Paige. I hope you enjoy your trip back home."

"Come here, baby," the man whispered. The creak of bedsprings was a blow to Paige's midsection that bent her at the waist.

With a click the telephone went dead.

Paige blinked hard as the receiver slipped out of her hand and fell with a thud to the floor. One needed breath and then another, she gulped each down as if she was starving for air. She felt fragmented, dazed. Pain echoed through her soul.

How could he do this to her again?

She slapped a palm over her mouth. This was all her fault. Why hadn't she listened to her mother? Why had she let him deceive her again?

Damn Nathan Cross to hell.

Damn the airplane that brought her to this wretched place.

Her hand fell to her side as she slowly rose, staring around the cottage where she and Nathan had loved and laughed. Lies. All lies. The bungalow was next on her list to curse when her sight fell upon the naupaka flower lying in two pieces on the table. How long had it been separated?

Her chest rose and fell rapidly. She felt dizzy, lightheaded, the air in her lungs seized.

Oh God. She couldn't breathe.

Her hands flew to her throat as tears streamed down her face. *Calm down. Get a hold of yourself.* But shudders whipped through her, making her body jerk uncontrollably. The need to get out of the cottage, out of Kauai and get away from the memories that were crashing in on her all at once was overwhelming. Everywhere she looked she saw Nathan's face. Felt his touch, his kiss.

Grasping a hold of the sliding glass doors, she pushed them wide and ran outside onto the balcony. Every gulp of oxygen stung her lungs, burned like she was swallowing fire. She moved from beneath the cover, and rain came down hard, stinging her skin, but she didn't care. The physical and mental agony all blended together into one big mass of nothingness.

In a blinding frenzy she swung open the gate and started down the wrought-iron steps. Her foot slipped. She fell down two steps, grappling for the banister for support. When she finally touched ground, she didn't stop running. Mud squished through her toes. Before she knew it, cold stone was beneath her feet. The angry ocean below called to her, and she fled in its direction.

The natural steps were slippery, but she didn't care. Not until a loud thunderclap shook the very ground. Her heart stuttered as the rock beneath her feet shifted, throwing her off balance. A squeak of surprise, of terror, slipped from her trembling lips. She attempted to offset her weight, leaning the other way, but failed. Her arms flailed. Face first, she fell into the sticky mud.

Before she could rise, a loud rumble sounded. The roar grew louder and louder, like the earth would open up and swallow her, and then there was an eerie silence. As she fought to stand, the image of a volcano erupting popped into her mind.

Was there a volcano on Kauai? Oh God. She couldn't remember. And if so, how close to the cottage?

The thought of spewing red-hot lava made her claw desperately at the gooey mud. If she could make it to the rock shelves, she could pull herself to safety. The now-soiled robe was hindering her movement. Her modesty was the least of her worries. She shrugged out of the wrap, laid it before her and crawled atop. It began to slip down the cliff, but not before her fingertips grasped the sharp edge of a rock. Using all her strength, she pulled herself onto the stone. Quickly and carefully, she stood.

She breathed a sigh of relief, but it was short lived.

The ground moved again. This time the force was so great it pitched her several feet from safety. She barely had time to brace herself for impact before the rolling noise began once more. She looked up to see the hillside above her shift and the side give way. An avalanche of mud, rock, trees and debris barreled toward her.

Fear was like a living substance engulfing her. Her feet and hands clawed through the sludge, fighting to get to the steps before it was too late. Frantically, she grabbed for the stone, the tips of her fingers touching the cold rock, but the pull of the slick mud surrounding her swept her up in the flow, carrying her with incredible speed down the cliff.

Whether it was training or a survival instinct, she curled her body, throwing her arms over her head for protection. As she slid farther down the incline, the debris mixed in the sandy mire scraped and scratched her limbs. The thick substance sucked her deeper within its grasp.

The rollercoaster ride ended two-thirds of the way down the mountainside, leaving Paige trapped up to her chest with one arm pinned to her side. Her legs wouldn't move. The pressure on her chest was suffocating. Nauseated and dizzy, she hung on the verge of unconsciousness. Maybe it was the most merciful thing that could happen to her, because the next wave of earth would bury her alive.

Nathan's palm struck the steering wheel of his Lexus sedan as he pulled onto the highway. It had taken Cami longer to fall asleep than he had planned. She had been so upset. Her sobs broke his heart.

Looking through the fast-moving windshield wipers, he curled his fingers tightly around the wheel. "Damn this rain and damn you, Sylvia," he snarled.

Cami had taken her mother's disappearance hard. Even more devastating was that the bitch left without saying goodbye. It nearly killed him when his daughter had claimed her mother's leaving was his fault. Maybe she was right, but he couldn't let that woman back into his life. He just couldn't, not even for Cami. He briefly squeezed his tired eyes closed, opening them as he approached a curve in the road. He jerked the wheel and tires squealed as the car skidded sideways around the turn.

"Fuck." Anxiety knotted his stomach. "Pull it together."

Nathan needed to talk to Paige in person, assure her that things were good between them, and then get back to Cami. Hopefully, Paige would understand. His place right now was with his child. If she woke up during the night and found him gone, it would crush her. He couldn't do that to her.

An image of Paige's crestfallen expression when he had tossed her the Hummer keys rose in his mind. Her expression had been one of disbelief and then pain. But he didn't know what else to do. He hadn't wanted her exposed to Sylvia any longer than necessary. The woman had a way of drawing blood with just a look.

Nathan glanced at the radio clock. "Sonofabitch." It was almost midnight, minutes before Christmas Eve. So busy with Cami, he'd forgotten to call Paige. When he had, the telephone had been busy. Hopefully he hadn't blown it. She had to be really upset to call her mother this late at night. He steered the car off the road and headed toward the cottage. Before he'd left the house he had tried once more to call her, only to receive no answer. There wasn't a doubt in his mind he would owe Paige a shitload of apologies, if she would even accept them.

In the distance he could see the lights of the cottage. "Please God, let her be there." If not, he had no choice but to follow her to the airport, because he wasn't letting her go this time. As he turned in front of the bungalow, his anxiety rose. Braking, he jammed the car into park and was out of the vehicle in a flash. He wasted no time making his way to the front door and pushed it open.

Lights flashed from the television that played softly, but other than that there were no signs of Paige. He rushed into the bedroom and then the bathroom, but no Paige.

"This can't be happening." When he reentered the living room he noticed the glass doors of the veranda were wedged wide. As he headed for the balcony, he saw the naupaka flower lying on the table in two pieces and it drew him up short. Had she separated the flowers?

His throat tightened. "Paige." He stared into the moonlit night. Was she standing in the dark thinking the worst?

Moving toward the balcony, he flipped the switch and light flooded the area. On a cursory look he didn't see her, so he stepped outside.

No Paige.

The wrought-iron gate clanked, drawing his attention. Maybe she had gone down to the beach. Before he reached the stairs the deck creaked, and then it shook with a vengeance, throwing his weight to one side. He tensed, fighting to gain his footing, when a loud moan similar to a nail forced from a board slithered up his spine. In a heartbeat the sound turned into a deafening rumble. The floor quaked again and the awning swayed. It felt as if the whole damn house was coming apart at the seams.

"What the hell—" Acid churned in his stomach. "Paige!"

Without a second thought he started down the staircase. "Paige!" The iron steps were slick, and twice he almost lost his footing. Trepidation built with each hastened step. He had to find her.

As he touched ground, sandy mud oozed over his sandals. The sticky stuff tugged at his feet, slowing his pace, but he continued to wade through the mire, heading for the stone steps which led to the ocean and hopefully Paige.

Thankfully the moon bled through the clouds, lighting his way. He took one more step and then froze, the sight chilling him to the bone. Half the mountainside was torn away. Even the steps had been disturbed, some lying crooked, some gone. Yet more importantly no shadowy form stood upon the beach looking out at the angry ocean crashing against the shore.

Desperately, he scanned the cliffside. The majority of vegetation was uprooted, trees lying on their side or covered in thick mud. He looked farther down the mountainside. Something moving caught his eye, and the breath he held escaped in a single gush. He felt the blood drain from his face. Paige was buried chest deep in the mud.

"Paige!" His feet moved on their own down the unstable steps. He literally had to jump from one platform to the next, nearly losing his footing. With the instability of the ground he knew he had to get to her, now.

Then the rumbling started anew. The teeth-grinding sound grew louder and louder until it exploded with a deafening crack that shook the very ground he stood on. Nathan glanced in the direction of the cottage. In slow motion, the veranda swayed, creaked. The support beams beneath the roof broke in two as if they were toothpicks flicked away, and the roof collapsed with a powerful bang. As the debris fell, what was left of the mountainside below began to shift and move, a slow, viscous flow at first down the slope that gathered speed on its descent— straight for Paige.

She screamed. The terror in her raucous cry ripped

through him. She must have seen him because she desperately waved one arm high in the air.

He had only seconds before the mire covered her completely.

"Paige! Hold on, baby, I'm coming." Thankfully, she was close to the rock shelf that he made his way down, slipping several times. The threat of falling into the treacherous flow slowed his pace. If he joined her, he would be no help.

As close as he was able to get to her, Nathan fell to his hands and knees on the cold, hard rock and extended his hand. The sight of her familiar shape lost in the mud covering her was gut-wrenching. "Paige. Baby. Hold on."

God. Please help him.

"Nathan." Her scratchy voice was a whisper over the ocean and the noise from the mudslide.

Their fingertips touched. Her muddy hand slipped through his. He had to get closer. Get a better hold. He leaned dangerously forward and was about to circle his fingers around her wrist when the avalanche of mud struck. Within a heartbeat it swallowed her up.

He screamed her name, but the nightmare continued as the flow whisked her away from him. Her muffled cry was the last thing he heard, before she disappeared below the dark surface.

His feet slid from beneath him as he tried to stand. Instead, he ended up rolling down several of the stone steps. Sharp rock bit into his rib cage, ripping at his flesh. Pain splintered in all directions, but it didn't slow his descent. When he found his footing, he ran down the remainder of the stairs.

Where was she?

The devastation around him was hard to comprehend. He

threw himself down on the beach and began to claw through the debris and mud. Frantically, he searched for Paige. Each time he came up empty-handed his heart sank a little deeper. He had to find her.

His fingers circled something and he yanked, only to dislodge a branch. He tossed it aside and dug harder, faster. His heart beat out of control when he grasped something slippery. It was her arm. He was sure of it. Using his other hand, he doubled his hold and pulled with all his might, but there was no give. Blinded by tears he hadn't realized he wept, he continued to paw at the goo until he had her head and upper body uncovered. Her eyes were closed. She wasn't moving.

The cry he heard was his own.

He looped his arms beneath her armpits, and with a powerful tug he tore her free. The strength and momentum tossed them both backwards. She landed hard against his chest.

"Paige," he said breathlessly.

She didn't respond.

He fought to find a pulse, but it was useless with the mud caking her naked body. Without delay, he rolled her off him and got to his feet, before picking her up and carrying her to the ocean.

Water splashed against his ankles as he waded deeper. Submerging them both in the cool waters, he worked to dislodge the mud from her face, mouth and nostrils. Even when he had cleared her airways, she was nonresponsive to his endeavors. He looked at her motionless chest, before leaning close to her mouth in an attempt to feel her breath.

Nothing. Her head wobbled listlessly as the angry waves beat against her lifeless body.

"God no," he cried out. He couldn't live without her.

"Breathe."

With two fingers to her throat, he felt for a pulse. Nothing. God, please help him. He had never felt for a pulse. Hell he didn't even know if he was in the right place. He tried again, still receiving no heartbeat. "Paige, please." His chest squeezed. He couldn't lose her again, not like this.

He ran toward the beach and laid her flat on her back, before falling to his knees. Hands shaking, he felt for a pulse once again.

Nothing.

One hand over the other, he placed them in the middle of her chest and started to bear down when he felt her chest rise beneath his touch. Her lips parted and she inhaled, crying out.

The sting of tears burned his eyes. His laughter was one of joy, short-lived when he pulled her into his arms. The painful scream she released made him loosen his grip.

"Hurt," she croaked.

He glanced up at the partially washed-away stone stairway. There was no way he could carry her up there, much less make it himself. "Shit." What the hell was he to do? Why hadn't he thought to grab his cell phone?

The lights of another cottage about a half a mile down the beach caught his eyes.

"Baby, I need to get help." If she had broken ribs or internal bleeding, carrying her might aggravate her wounds. The truth was he could move faster if he left her behind, although the thought didn't sit well with him. Still, he had no other choice. "Rest here. I promise I'll be back as soon as I can."

He didn't wait for a response before jumping to his feet and breaking into a full run. Somewhere down the stairs or in the ocean he had lost a sandal. He paused briefly to remove the other shoe as it hindered his speed. Barefoot, he continued.

The rock shelf leading to the cottage was slick. Several times he slipped, barely righting his balance before he took another step. Thankfully, the side of the mountain to this cottage was hardly disturbed from the excessive rain. As he topped the cliff, his thighs burned and so did his lungs, but it didn't slow his pace. Relentlessly he continued, heading for the staircase that led to the balcony. He didn't stop until he was standing before the sliding glass doors.

He peered in. A couple snuggling on the couch startled when he pounded on the glass.

A man dressed in only pajama bottoms stood and moved angrily toward Nathan. "What the hell do you want?" A petite dark-haired woman eased behind him.

"9-1-1," Nathan breathed. "Mudslide. Need help."

The man opened the glass doors as the woman went straight to the telephone.

Nathan bent over, sucking air into his lungs. "Half a mile..." he pulled in another breath, "...down the beach. Hurry."

The man started to speak, but Nathan had already spun around, heading down the wrought-iron stairs once again. His feet flew across the stone shelves. Each second that passed he prayed for Paige. She had to be okay. Mud squished between his toes as he stepped upon the beach and hit a full run.

Her shadowy form lay on the sand, waves caressing her feet. She hadn't moved. Naked and draped in moonlight, she looked like she had washed up on the beach. The scene sent shivers up his spine.

Alive, whispered through his mind. She had to be alive.

Out of breath and drenched with sweat when he arrived, Nathan could see that her eyes were closed. Fear squeezed his chest. When he stood before her, he dropped to his knees. "Paige." She didn't stir, so he repeated her name. He could detect no signs of breathing.

He reached out and noticed that his hand trembled. Her skin was clammy as he touched her and gave her a gentle shake.

She moaned softly. Her eyelids fluttered, but didn't open.

If only he hadn't sent her away. Guilt flooded his senses. His arms ached to hold her, but if she had injuries he wasn't aware of he could do more damage. Quickly, he pulled his T-shirt over his head and laid it across her exposed body. The garment was wet, but at least it would give her some semblance of decency when help arrived. Then he gathered her hand in his and waited.

Chapter Twelve

The scent of antiseptic hung heavy in the air while the ocean roared in Paige's head. That couldn't be right. She struggled to discern the two conflicting impressions, but her mind felt foggy, disconnected. She attempted to raise her eyelids, but they seemed glued together. Even the breath she inhaled fought against her and stung her lungs. Not to mention it hurt like hell. Anxiety crawled across her skin, making her aware of the bindings surrounding her.

She whimpered, icy fear taking a hold of her.

Trapped.

No. She had been trapped. Where? When? The memory seemed so close to her fingertips, but lay just out of her reach. Either way, she knew she had to get out of there or she would die.

"Try to remain calm, Dr. Weston." The tender words cut through the loud, hollow sound surrounding her, but not the terror that surged through her veins.

She couldn't move. So cold. The shiver that shook her made her teeth rattle. "Help me." Her mouth opened, but the scratchy, unrecognizable voice that emerged wasn't hers. She cried out again.

"You're safe, Dr. Weston. Please hold still. The test will be through in another minute or so."

"Test?" No. That couldn't be right. "Help me." She pried her eyes open but still couldn't see a thing.

"Do you know where you are, Dr. Weston?"

"Trapped." Her pulse felt like it would leap from her chest. "Dying."

"Oh, honey." Sympathy and concern softened the woman's tone. "You're neither trapped nor dying. You're at Wilcox Memorial."

"Hospital?" She choked. Her throat ached, felt swollen. The weight on her chest made it hard to inhale, or was she hyperventilating? Each breath was rapid and ragged.

"Yes. I'm performing an MRI on you. Now if you will remain still, the test will be done shortly and then we can chat."

She was in a magnetic resonance imager? Why?

The knowledge she was in a hospital helped to put her at ease, at least a little. Now if she could only patch her scattered memories together that lay in fragments in her mind. For some damn reason evil laughter and a child's tears popped into the dark recesses of her head, followed by Nathan's handsome face. When she felt a jolt, the image faded almost as quickly as it had materialized. Her heartbeat picked up speed as the hard surface beneath her shifted. A squeal left her trembling lips.

Oh God. It was happening again.

Her fingers curled into fists, but she felt helpless, unable to move.

"I'm right here," the woman said. Her touch was gentle and warm on Paige's arm.

"What's going on? I can't move or see." If only she could sit up and look around, maybe this feeling of dread would go away.

"You have salve in your eyes. The mud scratched them up pretty badly."

"Mud?"

"Do you remember being in a mudslide?" the woman asked.

Paige's head hurt as if a whirlwind swept through, stirring up pieces of her memory and throwing them together. "No. Yes."

Sylvia had called. Nathan wasn't coming, but he did, or had she just imagined it?

"What are my injuries?" Even as she asked the question she wondered if her remembrance of Nathan was real, and if so why he wasn't here with her now.

The woman chuckled. "Just like a doctor." She patted Paige's arm. "Let me get you back to a room. Your young man has been as crotchety as an old bear to see you. I had to literally throw him out while I performed the test. Dr. Waters should be in shortly and he'll discuss his findings."

It wasn't a dream. Nathan had been at the cottage and was here. Did he come to say goodbye? A pang in her forehead stole the place of the thought. She fought the pressure that felt like her head was wedged in a vise. Additional voices rose in the room. She froze when something or someone raised the hard surface she laid on into the air. As her body floated sideways and then was lowered, a tight cry pushed from her trembling lips. She recognized the fresh smell of clean sheets that were pulled up around her. Then something warm, a blanket, was placed over her body. Wheels creaked. The bed she must be lying on began to move. A door opened and the sound of pounding footsteps approached.

"Thank God." Tension deepened Nathan's voice. "Baby, are you okay?" He touched her hand and moisture bloomed behind her closed eyelids.

She choked on the tears barreling to the surface, but didn't let them fall. She managed a simple, "Yes," even though she wasn't sure. She still couldn't move or see. It hurt to breathe.

There was no doubt in her mind that she had a broken rib or at least a couple bruised ones. And Nathan was beside her.

"I'm sorry I wasn't there." He held her hand as someone pushed the bed down the hall.

She didn't know how to respond or feel.

He raised her palm to his mouth, and she felt his lips, warm and moist, against her wrist. "You scared me to death. Why didn't you answer the phone? Why did you try to go down to the beach in the rain?"

"Why?" Her voice pitched as the hold she had on her control began to crumble. "Sylvia called—"

"What?" Anger bled through his single word.

Paige swallowed the emotion tightening her throat. "She said you weren't coming." She licked her dry, chapped lips. "I thought I heard you in the b-background." Tears slid down her cheeks, a couple nestled in her ears. The bed swayed, turning one way while her mind went another. Nausea built in her stomach. She fought the sensation.

Nathan remained quiet until the motion of the bed stopped and the door creaked closed. "Damn her. I'm so sorry. That bitch left without telling Cami goodbye. I couldn't leave, not until I had her calmed down." He paused before adding, "I can't believe she called you."

"It doesn't matter," Paige heard herself say as she attempted to pull herself together.

"It matters to me. She swore to make my life a living hell and she almost succeeded." He grew quiet. "When the mud swept you away, I thought for sure that I'd lost you."

Nathan had screamed her name, Paige remembered now. Then there was nothing else until she woke up during the MRI test. Maybe it was her way of blocking out the devastation of the event. Maybe she couldn't bear him saying goodbye.

"What time is it?" she asked, wanting to vanquish the dreaded thought from her mind.

"Seven in the morning," he responded.

The door creaked again and she pried her eyelids open. Blinking, she made out two shadowy forms coming through the doorway.

"Nathan," Dr. Waters said. "How is our patient doing?"

"I'm in one piece, or at least I think I am. Why can't I move? What's the damage to my eyes?"

"Easy does it, young lady." Dr. Waters chuckled. "No internal bleeding or broken bones, but you have a nasty bruise on the left side of your rib cage." As he continued, the nurse began to undo the brace around her neck. "You ingested some mud and water. I'd suspect that you're having trouble breathing and have a nasty sore throat." Velcro ripped apart as the nurse undid her wrists and knees. "Antibiotics have been started in case of infection. You have some cuts from debris that had to be stitched. Let's roll her to the side and get the uncomfortable board from beneath her." The two of them manually wielded her on her side and extracted the spinal board.

"What about my eyes?" She couldn't bear to lose her sight. Her career would be over. Eased onto her back, she flinched as someone wiped a dry cloth over her eyes. She blinked again. Dr. Waters' face was still blurry, but at least she could make out some of his features. She gave up trying to recognize the nurse beside him.

"Your eyes are scratched and agitated, but should heal without a problem as long as we keep the infection under control. Now, let's talk about your state of mind."

"My state of mind?" What the hell was he talking about?

"I spoke to Connie in x-ray."

Oh shit.

"What happened?" Nathan asked.

"Nothing," Paige assured him. She had been confused, that's all.

Dr. Waters frowned. "We'll talk about it later. What I'd like to do is keep you overnight for observation."

"It isn't necessary. I just want to go home." But she didn't have a home to go to, not here on Kauai. She fought tears that threatened to fall.

"She'll stay put and won't fight you." The no-argument tone in Nathan's voice irritated her, until he added, "I want her in top shape for Christmas on Lotus Point."

He was taking her to his parents' island for Christmas? That meant that he had chosen her over Sylvia, but what about Cami? What would his daughter think? Say?

"I can't promise she'll be in top shape. Rest and sleep is what she needs now." Dr. Waters patted her on the hand. "No turkey or ham, maybe some mashed potatoes and gravy. Better yet, a liquid diet would probably suffice. I've ordered you something to help you sleep."

The nurse quietly left the room.

Paige started to decline the medicine, when Nathan said, "Whatever you think is necessary." She scowled at him. His smile was so heartfelt she didn't comment any further. Besides, she knew sleep was best for her.

"I'll check in later. If I don't get home now my wife and grandchildren will skin me alive. The kids are climbing the walls. It's tradition in our family to open one present on Christmas Eve." Dr. Waters shook Nathan's hand before he turned to leave.

Nathan leaned over the bed and kissed her tenderly on the lips. "I'm so thankful you're okay."

She loved the way he unconsciously drew circles atop her hand. "Was anyone else hurt?"

"No." He took a seat in the chair next to the bed. "While you were x-rayed and tested, I contacted the hotel's nightshift to be sure. They'll contact a local engineering company sometime today for an emergency survey of each cottage with a rock shelf."

A surveyor on Christmas day would probably cost him an arm and a leg, but a lawsuit would be even more expensive.

"When the ground firms, the steps will be reinforced throughout. Mudslides after this amount of rain are always a possibility, so I would suspect beach patrol will be posting signs. At the hotel, each guest will be contacted personally of the potential danger." As he raised his arm, threading his fingers through his hair, she noted that he was wearing a pair of green scrubs. "I can't believe this happened."

"It's over and I'm okay." She tried to reassure him.

"I could have lost you."

"But you didn't."

Sylvia had lied. Even Cami's unhappiness hadn't changed the fact that he wanted Paige, and the knowledge filled her with a peace she couldn't remember having in a long time.

The nurse returned. She smiled at both of them as she swathed the vee in the IV tube with an alcohol pad, before sticking a hypodermic needle into the opening. "You should feel the effects of the medicine shortly." She slipped a blood pressure cuff around Paige's arm. The machine made a humming sound and the cuff began to tighten.

Paige's eyelids felt heavy. She closed her eyes as the nurse finished taking her vitals. "How is Cami?" A thermometer was shoved into her mouth, silencing her.

"She and Janis will swing by here before leaving for the island. I need to talk to her. Make her understand why I won't be spending the day with them."

The nurse extracted the thermometer, and Paige forced her eyelids open. "You don't have to stay with me. I'll be okay."

"I want to be here when you fall asleep and wake up."

"That's kind of you, but—"

"Don't argue with me," he said firmly.

The nurse typed a few things into a computer and then she slipped out the door, closing it softly behind her.

Paige lost her battle when her eyelids slid closed again. "What about their safety? The ocean?"

"Except for a few lingering clouds, the newscaster said the storm is over."

"Thank God," she breathed, drifting into slumber.

For the longest time Nathan watched the gentle rise and fall of Paige's chest as she slept. Even though the doctor had said she'd be all right, he didn't feel right leaving her. Her face remained pale. Damn. Her bloodshot eyes had looked horrible. She had bruises all over her body. He cursed when he saw the stitches on her right forearm and knew there was a matching set on her left knee.

Sonofabitch. He should have been with her. He should have called her immediately after Sylvia left and all of this could have been avoided.

Damn that woman. He could only imagine what the witch said to Paige. Clearly his ex planned to make good on her threat. Of course, the man Paige heard in the background was probably one of Sylvia's many boyfriends. She adored attention and sought it wherever she could.

A light knock on the door turned his head. Cami peeked in, and he waved her and Janis in. His daughter crawled into his lap. Her troubled gaze was pinned on Paige. Janis remained near the door.

"Is she dead?" Cami asked.

"No, honey. She's sleeping."

"She looks dead."

He could see how a four-year-old would think that given the condition Paige was in. "Cami, I know this is hard for you to understand, but Paige is going to be a part of our lives from now on. I'm going to marry her. She'll be living with us."

Her bottom lip protruded. "I want Mommy," she whimpered. Tears misted her blue eyes.

"I know, and you'll always have your mommy. You'll also have Paige. Remember she fixed your foot? You liked her then, didn't you?"

Cami's troubled expression was heartbreaking. "Yes, but I want Mommy."

He didn't need to belabor the point. In time Cami would come to love Paige. His only hope was that Sylvia would someday be the mother Cami wanted and needed. "Janis and you are going to Papa's and Nana's house. I'll join you tomorrow. Okay?"

She cocked her head. "Do I get to open my presents?"

It was amazing how quickly a child's attention could go from one thing to another. Remembering the tradition that Dr. Waters observed, Nathan said, "You can open one tonight. But you have to wait on the others until Paige and I arrive Christmas morning. Is that a deal?"

She sat straight up in his lap. "Two," she blurted. "Two presents."

"One," he said, but crumbled like a week-old Christmas cookie when she pushed out that bottom lip again. "Okay, two, but no more than that." She started to climb off his lap, and he swatted her butt playfully.

She giggled as she ran to Janis.

"I'm sorry, Janis."

"Nathan, it's no trouble. I hope Dr. Weston will be all right." She hung her head. She'd been with the family long enough for him to detect that something wasn't right.

"What's wrong?" he asked.

When she raised her gaze to meet his, there were tears in her eyes. "I don't have anywhere to go," she choked.

He got up from his chair and approached the young woman. He didn't think twice about wrapping his arms around her. "Paige will love you as we do. You don't have to ever worry about not having a family. We're your family."

She glanced toward Paige. "Will she feel the same?"

"There isn't anyone as loving and caring as Paige. I'm sure the two of you will become BFFs immediately." She laughed at his effort to make a joke. Janis was always telling Cami that she was her BFF.

"Me too," Cami chirped. "I want to be her BFF too."

That was just what he was hoping for. "I'm sure all three of you will be best friends forever as soon as she's feeling better. Now get out of here and go help Nana with tomorrow's preparations. Make sure you don't drink all the eggnog."

"Yuck." Cami pinched her mouth.

Before Janis intertwined her fingers with Cami's, she glanced over a shoulder. "Thank you." Her expression was one of appreciation. As the door swung shut behind them, the blonde nurse returned.

"Sleeping?" Her nametag introduced her as Sally.

"Yes." He stepped closer to Paige and looked down upon her. He loved her so much. "How long do you think she'll be out?" Paige didn't even stir when Sally activated the blood pressure cuff.

She held Paige's wrist while looking at her watch, silently counting. "Depends. It could be an hour or half the day."

"I need to run a couple of errands. If she wakes before I return, will you tell her I'll be here shortly?" He hated not to be there when she woke, but there was one thing in particular he had to do. He'd call his mother on the way and let her know additional company would be joining them.

"Of course I will," Sally said.

He leaned down and pressed his mouth to Paige's. "I'll be back," he whispered.

Chapter Thirteen

Groggy, Paige woke slowly. She attempted to stretch, work out the soreness, but only one arm rose. The other felt numb, pinned to her side like before. Air burst from her lungs in terrified gasps. Her eyes widened. She sucked in a wild breath. A quick scan of the hospital room should have eased her racing mind, but she couldn't hold on to the rational thought. Visions of her cemented in the sandy mud popped into her head.

Panic was only an inhale away when she felt something soft and silky beneath her fingers. She jerked her gaze down to her side. Instead of a sea of slush she saw Nathan. A wave of relief rushed over her. Sleeping in a chair, he was hunched over her bed atop her arm.

It took her several minutes to slow her heartbeat. When she did she eased her arm from beneath him and began to work the sensation back into her limb. As blood surged throughout, tiny pinpricks tingled against her skin. She fisted her fingers, flexing.

Something shiny caught her eye. Her jaw dropped. A band of gold sporting a brilliant diamond circled her finger.

For a moment, she didn't breathe, and then she gulped air into her lungs all at once. It was the engagement ring she'd returned to Nathan five years ago. He had kept the ring all this time.

Emotion bubbled up inside her. He did love her. She blinked to rid herself of the sudden tears clouding her eyes.

"Merry Christmas, Paige."

Her bewildered gaze snapped away from the ring to see Nathan staring at her. "Will you marry me?"

She pinched her eyelids together to stop the river of tears that threatened. When that didn't work, she opened her eyes and let the waterworks burst.

"You okay, baby?"

She nodded rapidly. Her voice was temporarily absent due to the knot the size of a golf ball in her throat.

His forehead furrowed. "Is that a yes?"

She didn't have time to answer before Dr. Waters entered. He took one look at her, and then Nathan. "Is everything all right?"

"Um. I'm not sure," Nathan responded, frowning.

Paige still couldn't speak. She simply raised her hand. The subtle light glistened off the diamond.

Dr. Waters smiled. "Wonderful. Congratulations to the both of you." He handed her several tissues, and she wiped her eyes and dabbed at her nose. "It looks to be a dandy Christmas. Let me take a listen to those lungs and we can get you out of this place." Nathan moved aside to allow the doctor to step nearer. He placed his stethoscope against her chest. "Sounds like that heart of yours is racing, but I think that can be expected at a moment like this." The bed moaned as he angled the head of her bed so he could place the stethoscope on her back. "How are you feeling this morning?"

Morning? She had slept the entire day and night away?

"Good," she croaked.

He flipped on a light, drawing it close, before he checked

her eyes. His touch was gentle, but thorough, as he continued to examine the rest of her injuries. "I think you're going to live." He patted her knee. "I want you to take it easy for the next couple days."

"She will," Nathan chimed in.

"Remember rest. Give your body..." he paused, "...and mind, time to heal."

How could Dr. Waters know the fear that lingered beneath the surface within her? Every time she closed her eyes she relived that night.

"You can't go through a traumatic event like this and not have aftereffects. Just be good to yourself. Take it slow. Now..." the doctor patted her leg, "...you two lovebirds get out of here." He patted her knee. "Oh. I expect your resume on my desk by New Year's. I'm anxious to close the position and add you to my staff." His warm smile comforted her. "Merry Christmas, you two."

"Merry Christmas," Paige and Nathan chimed at the same time.

Dr. Waters shook Nathan's hand before exiting the room. They were finally alone again.

Paige pushed into a sitting position, and every muscle in her body screamed in pain. "Yes," she groaned.

"What?" Nathan turned to her. A look of confusion tugged at his brows.

"Yes, I'll marry you."

His mouth rose in a crooked smile. With four large steps he closed the distance between them. "That's what I needed to hear." He gingerly wrapped his arms around her. His kiss was even more cautious. "What do you say we get out of this place? I know Cami will be pacing the halls waiting to open the rest of her presents."

Cami? In Paige's happiness she'd almost forgotten about his daughter, the one who had screamed at her to get out of her house. "I don't want to ruin Cami's Christmas. Maybe you could take me back to the cottage." The thought sent shivers up her spine. She really wasn't ready to go back there.

"The cottage isn't safe. You don't remember the balcony collapsing?" He frowned again.

Everything had happened so quickly. "No." She didn't recall that detail.

"You can't go back there. I don't know how stable the dwelling is. Besides, Cami and I've talked. She knows that you're joining us for Christmas." He brushed his lips across hers once more. "And that you'll be living with us."

"Sounds like you've been busy." She couldn't help wondering what the fallout had been from that conversation. Still, she gathered some comfort from his grin. His face literally beamed with something more. "What?"

"You'll see when we get to the island. Let's get you dressed."

She glanced around the room for the clothes she'd come in with. Heat flushed her face when she remembered she had been naked, her robe lost in the mud. "I don't have anything to wear."

He pulled the bags of clothes she had purchased when they went shopping together from beneath the bed. "I hope I got everything you need." He laid the sacks on her bed.

Nathan had a clean change of clothes. Instead of the green scrubs, he wore a pressed pair of khakis and a dress shirt. He even had loafers on.

She began to dig through the clothes and toiletries. "You really have been busy." She extracted a short red evening dress and matching heels. They would be perfect for Christmas. She picked up a mirror and gazed into it, cringing. "Oh my God. I look like I've been mugged." Scratches, bruises and one black eye marred her face. Not to mention, her hair was a mess. Thankfully it was free of mud. But it was her inflamed eyes streaked with red that glowed as if she were a demon.

"You're beautiful." Nathan ran a brush through her tangles, pulling gently.

"Even my hair roots are sore."

"I'm sorry." He stopped, and she felt badly for complaining.

She touched his hand. "Don't be. Please continue. I love it when you touch me."

He chuckled. "Is that an invitation?"

"Maybe tonight." Of course, she didn't know what to expect at his parents' island. Would they have separate rooms? Lord, she hoped not. She needed to fall asleep in his arms, better yet wake up in them. But the last time she had visited his parents' home, they had given her and Nathan separate rooms. She might as well get used to the idea. Besides, it wasn't right sharing a bed with Nathan, knowing his daughter was right down the hall. Especially so soon after Cami had caught them in bed together.

After he finished brushing her hair, she stood up and shrugged out of the hospital gown. He helped her fasten her bra. She reached for a pair of lacy red panties.

"Do you have to wear those?" he grumbled.

"Yes." She slipped them on. The dress was short. A gust of wind or bending over too much would raise her hem and everyone would know she was naked beneath.

"I like you without panties."

So did she, but there was no way she would spend the day

with his daughter and parents without being fully dressed. He knelt and helped her with her heels.

Excitement built as the nurse came with the dismissal papers and wheelchair. In less then an hour she would be face-to-face with Nathan's family. She only half-listened to the directions Sally spouted, before she signed the forms.

What would his parents say about their engagement?

What would Cami say?

Paige had never been so afraid of one child as she was Nathan's daughter. She took a seat in the wheelchair and her anxiety rose. She glanced at Nathan walking beside her. "Maybe we should wait to announce our engagement."

"Cold feet?" he asked.

"No. I'm just worried about Cami."

"I've handled everything." He sounded so confident she didn't bring the subject up again.

When they exited the hospital there was a black limousine parked out front. The second the driver saw them he opened the back door.

"Ours?" she asked.

Nathan nodded. "Nothing but the best for my fiancée."

She liked the sound of that.

"Congratulations," Sally said.

"Thank you," Paige and Nathan said in unison.

She climbed in and he followed her inside the big car. As the driver got behind the wheel and started the vehicle, Nathan popped the top on a bottle that had been chilling in a bucket of ice. He poured the effervescent drink into two wineglasses and handed one to her.

"To us," he said.

She took a sip and choked. "Apple juice?"

"No alcohol with your medication."

"Don't tell me, you're going to be a doting husband."

"If you'll allow me to. Come here."

She snuggled close to him. He felt so good—so right. She yawned, closing her eyes.

"Mr. Cross, did you want to make a stop at the pharmacy?" the driver asked.

Nathan pulled Paige closer into his embrace. "Yes. Thank you." She slept soundly. He could hear her light breathing, see her chest rise and fall with each inhale/exhale. He loved the way she held on to him unconsciously.

The pharmacy wasn't far and the hospital had called in Paige's prescriptions to save them time. In minutes they were back on the road. He had gotten word earlier that Paige's mother and sister had arrived at the airport. They would be meeting them at the dock for the ride over to the island.

Needless to say, Evelyn was anxious to see her daughter since he had called her about the accident yesterday. The weather had postponed their trip until late last night. It took every negotiating skill he had to keep her from calling Paige and ruining his surprise, but Susan had jumped on his side and assisted him.

As they drove around a corner, he could see Evelyn and Susan waiting on the dock. The minute the limo pulled to a stop they rushed over.

"Paige, baby, it's time to get up." He kissed her forehead.

"What?" She sounded so groggy, tired.

Paige became wide awake when Evelyn jerked open the door and leaned over him. "Sweetheart, are you okay?" The woman's light perfume, something citrusy, filled the enclosed space. He pressed his back against the seat to allow her more access to her daughter.

"Mom?" Paige glanced at him. "Did you do this?"

He nodded.

Evelyn's eagle eyes scanned over her daughter, frowning each time she encountered a bruise. Tears built in her eyes when she saw the numerous stitches. "Nathan Daniel Cross. You were supposed to keep my daughter safe."

Susan tugged her mother's arm, pulling her backward. "Come on, Mom. At least let them get out of the car." She gave him an apologetic shrug as he exited to assist Paige. When she stepped out, both her mother and sister bombarded her with hugs and kisses. It was like a gaggle of geese all talking at the same time. That didn't last long before the tears began to fall.

Then an uncomfortable silence ensued.

Evelyn raised Paige's hand. "Is this what I think it is?" Apprehension simmered in the older woman's eyes.

Nathan moved beside Paige. He snaked his arm around her shoulders protectively.

She nodded before answering, "Yes."

Susan snatched Paige's hand from her mother's and stared at the ring. "I've always adored this ring." Yet even her expression held a measure of unrest. "Congratulations." True joy was missing in the felicitation.

Immediately, he went into defensive mode. "I know what you're thinking. Maybe this is too fast—"

"You think?" Susan clapped a hand over her mouth, removing it before she uttered, "I'm sorry, Paige."

Paige looked exhausted, but still she mustered a smile. "Don't be. It's what I want."

173

"We want," he added. The captain of the cruiser waved at him. "Let's get going so Captain Dean can get to his family." They lived on Lotus Point and worked exclusively for the Crosses.

Nathan led the way aboard the F46 Sealine Cruiser. Without a word, each of them took a seat on the L-shaped seating portside. Corky, Captain Dean's eldest son, sometimes served as cabin boy. Dressed in a Hawaiian print shirt, white board shorts and deck shoes, he approached. His long dark hair looked as if he could use a haircut.

"May I get you something to drink?" he asked politely.

"Thank you, but I'm good," Evelyn said. A smile crept across her face as she stared out over the ocean. The water was calm. The sky was a vibrant blue. Only a couple clouds still hung around.

Susan scooted closer to Nathan. "Tell me this is for real?" She spoke softly. "She can't go through another letdown like before."

"You have nothing to worry about," he tried to assure her.

"You won't mind if I worry until I see it for myself?" she muttered.

"Not at all." If he had his way, he would have taken Paige straight to the justice of the peace and married her the minute she was released from the hospital.

Susan and her mother chatted during the twenty-minute ride, while Paige once again fell asleep. To make the ride smoother, he raised her into his lap, holding her close.

When they arrived at the island, his parents, Cami, Janis and a host of friends and family awaited them. Paige stirred, and he captured her first waking moment with a kiss. "We're here."

She yawned, moaning as if moving hurt. "I must be a mess."

"You're beautiful," he reassured her.

Hand in hand, they disembarked. He only released her to his father as he helped her to the dock. "Paige, it's such a pleasure to see you again."

She stepped carefully off the cruiser. "The pleasure is mine, Mr. Cross."

"Dan," he reminded her. "I heard what you did for the boy on the plane. Kudos to you, young lady." He shook her hand vibrantly.

Daniel Cross was a fit man at fifty-five. Six-two, there wasn't a gray hair on his dark head. He lived life to its fullest. Their island home was his baby.

Next, Paige was introduced to his Aunt Betty, her new husband, and a couple of cousins Nathan hadn't seen in some time. They spoke briefly before moving to the next person.

Nathan's mother, Naomi Cross, looked at them and smiled. The image of grace and elegance, she wore a chiffon dress. Not a hair out of place, her ebony hair combed in an updo. Always the perfect hostess. In truth, his mother was the financial genius to their wealth. She was bright and cunning when she needed to be.

"Oh my." Her startled cry made Paige lick her lips again as they approached. "Are you all right, dear?"

"Yes."

"I'm afraid to touch you," his mother said.

Nathan smiled when Paige leaned in for a hug. "Thank you for allowing my family to join yours for the holidays."

"I wouldn't have it any other way. We have a full day planned."

Nathan saw the weariness in Paige's face. "Mom, I think Paige needs a little rest before we overwhelm her with the frolics of the Crosses."

"Yes. Of course. How inconsiderate of me. Cami?"

The little girl peeked out from behind Janis. "Yes, Nana?" She ran to her daddy and they embraced.

"Can you please show Paige to your father's room? He needs to help your papa with the pig."

There was a moment of awkwardness and then Cami stepped forward. She stared up at Paige, who looked as if she would burst into tears at any moment. When his daughter reached for Paige's hand, Nathan breathed a sigh of relief, and he swore Paige did too.

"Nana said I should say I'm glad you're feeling better, Dr. Weston."

"From the mouths of babes," his mom murmured out of the corner of her mouth.

"Call me Paige."

"Nana, is that okay?" Cami yelled over her shoulder.

"Yes, dear." His mom stifled a chuckle.

"Can Janis come with us?" his daughter asked.

"Certainly," Paige responded.

"Janis, you can come too."

A grin rose on Janis's face as she joined them.

His mom greeted Evelyn and Susan. "I'll show both of you to your rooms and we can all convene in the parlor. Maybe we could chat before the celebration begins."

"Thank you for allowing us to barge in on your celebration," Evelyn said. "We do appreciate the opportunity to spend Christmas with Paige."

"Say no more. It's our pleasure."

As his mom walked off with Paige's family, his father approached. "Your mom has been scheming."

"Pardon me?"

"You should be prepared for anything today."

"Something you want to share with me, Dad?"

"Nope." He slapped his son on the back. "Just be ready for anything."

Nathan stood bewildered. One thing he and Paige didn't need was more surprises.

Chapter Fourteen

Paige looked down at the little girl holding her hand. None of them spoke, including Janis, as they headed for the big house. Perhaps *big* didn't appropriately describe the Crosses' mansion. It was more like a hotel. If she remembered right there were at least twenty bedrooms in the manor. Nathan's family's wealth was mind-boggling.

"Daddy says you're coming to live with us."

Every muscle in Paige's body tensed. Did she dare ask? "Would that be okay with you?"

When the child didn't answer immediately, Paige swallowed her silent cry of disappointment. The one child she wanted desperately to accept her only stared up at her with an unreadable expression.

Seconds felt like minutes until Cami spoke again. "He said we'd be BFFs."

Paige couldn't withhold her surprise. *Best friends forever.* That was one response she hadn't expected. Tears misted her eyes. "I'd like that."

"Janis too? Can she be our BFF too?"

Janis squared her shoulders. The fear of rejection on the young girl's face was hard to miss.

"Yes. Janis too."

The tension in Janis's shoulders eased, and she smiled.

Cami gave Paige's hand a jerk as she continued forward. "Okay."

"Okay?" she asked.

"Okay. You can move in with us."

Just like that? Lord. She had forgotten how accepting children could be.

As they entered the house, two massive fans spun slowly above them. The colonial columns at the end of the entryway reminded her of the southern mansions she had toured in New Orleans. Yet everything in this estate was fresh and new and elegant.

"Nana said we could ride the elevator." Cami released Paige's hand as she skipped around the corner. "Do you want to?"

Paige glanced at Janis. "Sure, that sounds like fun."

"She loves riding the elevator," Janis said softly. There was an awkward pause and then she cleared her throat. "Nathan said you wouldn't mind me staying on as Cami's nanny."

Turning the corner, Paige saw the elevator slide open and Cami race inside. She peeked out. "Hurry up, slowpokes."

Janis and Paige picked up the pace.

"The way Nathan speaks of you, you're part of the family, not a nanny." Paige didn't miss the emotion welling in Janis's eyes.

"I love them both. Nathan has been so good to me."

Paige grasped Janis's hand and squeezed it before letting her go. "I hope we can be BFFs soon."

The big grin on Janis's face was priceless. "Me too."

They stepped into the elevator and Cami pushed a button.

The doors moaned closed and the elevator began to move. The unsteady floor stole Paige's breath. A moment of dread paralyzed her.

Janis gave her a strange look. "You okay?"

"Yes." But she wasn't okay. Her hands shook and her knees felt weak, until Cami looked up at her and took her hand. The child's touch and show of caring helped to calm Paige's fear.

When the doors slid open, Cami gave her a tug and pulled her forward. "This way." Nathan's daughter giggled. "We have a surprise."

Janis's grin disappeared. "Cami! Uh. Remember what your Nana said."

"But BFFs don't keep secrets. You said so."

"Yes. But this is a little different. This is your Nana's surprise."

No more surprises. Paige had had enough this trip. "Anyone want to tell me what's going on?"

Janis didn't answer as she opened Nathan's bedroom door. When Paige entered, she could smell his essence as if he stood before her. God, she loved that man.

"Naomi asked that you open your present before you come downstairs." She pointed toward a box wrapped in white tissue paper lying upon the large bed.

"I want to see her open it." Excitement rang in Cami's voice.

"No. It's time that we allow Dr. Weston—"

"Paige. We're BFFs now."

Janis's mouth curved into a smile. She scooped Cami's hand in hers. "Paige needs a little time to herself."

Cami's chin drooped. She pinched her lips together.

"Let's go and count your presents. As soon as everyone is

settled, you'll be able to open them."

Cami jumped several times. "Yippee!"

Janis looked at Paige. "When you're ready, you can join us in the living room." She pulled the door closed behind her and Cami.

Paige released a weighted sigh. She was exhausted, mentally and physically. A soft knock on the door made her turn around.

The doorknob twisted and Naomi stuck her head in. "Decent?"

Paige chuckled. "Yes."

Her future mother-in-law stepped into the room, her sight pinned on the gift. "You haven't opened your present."

"Not yet. Would you like me to wait for the others?"

"No." Naomi's response was short. She sat on the bed. "Please. Open it now, and then we'll chat."

Paige moved across the room and picked up the gift. She ran a finger beneath the taped seam and the paper loosened.

"I hope you don't think that I'm being pushy or presumptuous, but both you and Nathan have been deprived long enough."

Paige raised the lid and moved aside the tissue paper to reveal a white chiffon gown. It looked like a wedding dress. Shocked, she stared at Naomi.

"I've made all the arrangements for the two of you to be married on the island—this evening."

Paige's jaw dropped. "Today?"

"Yes."

Anxiety skittered across her skin. "Does Nathan know about this?"

"Oh dear, you know the men of the family are the last to hear anything." She winked and smiled. "No. I wanted to speak to you first. I know what my son wants. He'd marry you in a heartbeat."

"But Cami—"

"She's aware of the plans. She's okay for now, but you'll have to have patience with her after her mother gets a hold of her." The smile she wore faded into a frown. Clearly, there was no love lost between Nathan's mother and his ex. "So, will you accept my present?"

"Thank you—"

"I hear a *but* coming."

"I need to speak with Nathan." What if this wasn't what he wanted?

"About what?"

Paige spun around to see Nathan walking through the door with their bags in his hands. "Speak to me about what?" He set their bags on the floor.

"I'll leave you two alone." Naomi rose from the bed.

"Mom?" Nathan grumbled.

She kissed him on the cheek, before she whispered, "She's a keeper, son." Standing at the door, she turned back to face them. "Don't be long. Cami has waited all morning to open her presents."

When the door closed behind his mother, Nathan turned to Paige. "Dad said she's up to something. I thought I'd come and warn you." He frowned. "I'm too late."

Paige was speechless.

"What did my mother say or do?"

Without a word she extracted the dress from the box and held it up for him to see.

"Beautiful. Looks like a wedding dress." He shot her a look of concern and a multitude of insecurities rushed through her mind.

"I'm sorry," he said. "She can be presumptuous at times. I'll inform her that you want to choose your own gown."

"I love the dress." And she did. It was a silk charmeuse strapless gown. Metallic embroidery, rhinestones, crystal beading and sequin design along the bodice were gorgeous accents. The chapel train in the back was simple but elegant. In fact, the gown was almost the image of the one Paige had chosen years ago. Naomi had remembered. A lump of emotion nearly released the tears she held back.

"Then what's the problem?"

She swallowed hard. "Your mother has offered the island for our wedding."

He shook his head. "That woman. Of course where we marry is up to you as well."

"No. I don't think you're getting the point here."

His frown deepened. "Which is?"

There was no other way to say it. "Your mom has arranged for us to be married this evening."

"She's what?" His voice dropped like a lead balloon.

"Married. Today." She spoke each word slowly.

There was a pregnant pause before he grinned like a schoolboy.

Goose bumps raced across her skin.

He reached for her, pinning the gown between them. "What did you say to her?"

"I said I had to speak with you."

He brushed his mouth lightly over hers, tickling her lips.

"Will you marry me tonight?"

Tonight? Was it possible that all her dreams could come true in less than eight hours?

"Yes," she said abruptly, before the voice of reason in her head could persuade her otherwise. She released the dress, and it slid between them as she threw her arms around his neck. "Yes. Yes. Yes."

Nathan captured Paige's mouth with his. She returned his passion, crying out when he hugged her a little too tight. He released her immediately. "I'm so sorry."

She ran her hands down his chest. "Don't be. I'm just a little sore."

How damn selfish was he? Here she had just been through a traumatic event and all he could think of was putting a ring around her finger as soon as possible. "Maybe we should delay the wedding."

She curled her fingers into his shirt and pulled him to her. "Not on your life, buddy."

Happiness rose inside him. This was one time his mother's interference was welcome. Tonight his one true love would be his forever. Gently, he reached for her and pulled her close. "I love you."

"I love you too."

He leaned in for another kiss.

When they parted she moved out of his embrace. "Give me a second to freshen up and we can watch Cami open her presents." She headed toward her bags, but he beat her to it.

"You need to take a nap," he insisted.

"I'm fine. Really. I want to be part of the celebration. Just let me freshen up."

He placed the bag on the big mahogany bed. The zipper hissed as she opened it and retrieved some cosmetics, a brush and other toiletries. "Won't take me but a second." She pivoted, heading toward the bathroom off his bedroom.

Nathan sat on the bed. His mother was amazing. Yet, in all honesty, he knew she had an ulterior motive. He'd lay a bet this quickie marriage was to close any doors to Sylvia's return.

Paige stepped out of the bathroom. Her makeup had been reapplied, and she wore a smile from ear to ear.

"Ready?" He stood and took her hand, leading her out of the room and down the hall.

From somewhere below they heard laughter. "It sounds like the celebration has begun." He pressed his lips to her forehead before they started down the stairs.

When they entered the living room all eyes were on them. Soft Christmas music played in the background. Paige tensed beneath his palm pressed to the small of her back.

"Daddy." Cami ran into his arms and he picked her up. "Can I open my presents now?"

He kissed her cheek and set her down. "Yes, princess."

When her feet hit the ground she literally dove beneath the tree, along with some of their younger guests. Janis was beside them to assist. Paige strolled over to her mother and sister, who sat on one of the three leather couches in the room. The room was cheery, designed for entertaining and comfort, down to the heap of decorative pillows on the floor for Cami and the other children.

The ripping of paper proceeded as the children began to tear their gifts open. A sea of colorful paper flew into the air. Ohs and ahs and laughter filled the room. Presents were passed out to everyone and the heap of paper grew taller. Even Paige looked as if she enjoyed herself. She watched Cami with a

185

tender expression on her face that squeezed his chest. He couldn't believe that the two most important people in his life were in the same room together. As his mother rose from where she sat, he realized that everyone in this room held a special place in his life. His mother looked from him to Paige with a single question in her eyes.

He nodded and she beamed from ear to ear. "I'd like to announce that my son and his lovely fiancée have agreed to a wedding tonight on the beach."

A roar of applause rose. He noted that Evelyn and Susan didn't appear surprised as they began to chat with Paige. No doubt his meddlesome mother had already discussed her plans with Paige's family. He strolled across the room and took a seat on the arm of the couch next to Paige. Cami quickly joined them on his lap.

He tapped her on the nose. "How did you ever keep such an important surprise?"

"Nana said I had to or I wouldn't get to open my presents."

He glanced at his mother. She shrugged as if she didn't know what the child was talking about, but he didn't miss the twinkle in her eyes.

"Daddy?"

He turned back around to his daughter. "Yes, Cami?"

"Does this mean you don't love Mommy anymore?"

The entire room fell silent.

Nathan held Cami tighter. He had never loved Sylvia, but his daughter didn't need to know the truth.

When he started to respond, Paige spoke up. "Cami, your daddy will always love your mommy for giving him such a special little girl."

The relief on Cami's face meant everything to him, and it

was all because of the beautiful woman beside him.

"Cami, I think there are two more gifts beneath the tree for my two BFFs," Paige said.

She jumped off his lap. "For me and Janis?"

Paige nodded.

Cami ran toward the tree, and Janis retrieved the two gifts Paige had purchased for them.

Nathan snaked his arm around Paige. "Thank you."

Together they watched Cami and Janis open Paige's presents.

Cami hugged the doll close to her chest. "Daddy, a new dolly."

Janis stood up and approached with a big grin on her face. "Thank you, Paige. A girl can never have too many bathing suits."

"You're welcome, Janis." Paige wished her a Merry Christmas and received a genuine hug from her before she rejoined Cami and the other children.

"Is this what you want?" Evelyn asked her daughter.

"It's all I have ever wanted, Mom."

"Then I suggest you get some rest before the big event. Susan and I will ensure everything is how you would prefer."

Evelyn and his mother nose to nose, not a pretty sight.

"Your mom is right, Paige. Give me a minute and I'll join you. I'll bring up some breakfast so you have something to eat before you climb into bed."

"I doubt she'll get any rest if you join her," Evelyn said bluntly.

"Mom!" Color rushed across Paige's cheeks. A few people within earshot chuckled.

"Susan can deliver your breakfast. I'm sure there's a lot to keep Nathan busy until this evening."

Evelyn was correct, but nothing more pressing than holding Paige in his arms while she slept. Yet by the firmness in his soon-to-be mother-in-law's face, he would not get that opportunity until tonight.

As they all stood, Nathan pulled Paige into his arms. "Tonight?"

She went on her tiptoes and kissed him softly. "Tonight."

This was one Christmas he would never forget.

Chapter Fifteen

A gentle breeze ruffled Paige's loose hair, threatening to dislodge the naupaka flower she wore, but she had no worries. This time the two halves were not left to fate or the gods. Her mother had ordered the flowers wired together. There was no way they were coming apart—ever.

The soft rhythm of the ocean surf played in the background as Paige stared deep into Nathan's eyes. "I promise to love you unconditionally, to support you in your goals, to honor and respect you, to laugh with you and cry with you, and to cherish you for as long as we both shall live." Beneath a vibrant sunset he finished the same vows he had prepared five years ago.

Friends and family stood behind them, the justice of the peace before them. The scent of salt and flowers hung in the air, but Paige had only one thing on her mind, becoming Nathan's wife.

"I take you, Nathan Daniel Cross, to be my husband, my partner in life and my one true love." A seagull squawked above them on its way to find a roosting place for the evening. "I will cherish our union and love you more each day than I did the day before." Which had already been the case throughout the years they were separated. "I will love you faithfully through good times and bad, regardless of the obstacles we may face together." She raised her hand and placed it in his. "I give you my hand, my heart, and my love, from this day forward, for as long as we both shall live."

He smiled, before mouthing *I love you.* The radiant look in his eyes wrapped her in a blanket of happiness as she repeated the same words.

The justice of the peace turned his attention to the audience. "As Paige and Nathan prepare to join their lives, it's important to understand that everyone present will play a vital role in their future. Thus we are here not only to witness their vows to each other, but also bestow upon them our blessing. I ask all present, do you bless this couple and pledge, now and forever, to support and strengthen their marriage by upholding Paige and Nathan with your love and concern?"

Paige waited with bated breath for that single voice beside her. When she heard Cami say, "I do," she smiled, basking in the precious moment.

"Then with the authority vested in me, I now pronounce you husband and wife. Nathan, you may kiss your bride."

She had never heard anything so wonderful in her life. As he took her into his embrace a tremor raced through her. His lips were gentle against hers, but his arms were firm as if he would never let her go. Her toes curled in the white sand beneath her feet. When the caress ended, the audience roared. Nathan and Paige turned around to flower petals being thrown in the air. Even Cami tossed a handful at them, and then she ran to her daddy. He raised her in one arm, while he held Paige close with the other.

She looked at the first row of seats where her mother and Susan stood. Both had tears in their eyes as they rushed toward her. Somehow in the midst of hugs and congratulations she and Nathan were separated.

"Honey, I've never seen you look so happy and vibrant," her

mother said.

"Bloodshot eyes and all?" Paige asked.

"Naomi's photographer will make all the necessary touches so that what you remember is the beauty of this evening minus the memories of that dreadful night," Susan assured her.

Her sister leaned into Paige, her eyes on Nathan. "You know he is rather yummy. I'm so happy for you."

Dressed in white pants and a short-sleeve silk shirt, he chatted with his aunt. As if he knew Susan and Paige spoke of him, he turned and smiled.

"That little girl of his is a charmer like her father. Any worries there?" Susan asked.

Paige didn't get an opportunity to answer. Her husband approached. God, that sounded wonderful. Her husband.

He intertwined his fingers with hers. "Ladies, if I could steal my wife for a minute or two." Without waiting for an answer he led her down the beach and away from the crowd. "Mom has arranged a big party, but if you're not up to it we can skip out after the cake is cut."

She grasped his other hand, pressing her body against his. "I think I'd like to get you alone as soon as possible." The heat of arousal warmed her body. Her silky gown rubbed back and forth seductively over her taut nipples as she inched closer.

He made that little growl that she had come to love just before he captured her mouth in a hungry caress. His erection began to harden between them and she wiggled against him. The next time they made love it would be as husband and wife.

When they parted, his mother was approaching. "There's enough time for that later, you two. The sun is setting and I want more pictures before it's dark."

As they began to walk toward the crowd, Naomi cleared her

throat. "Nathan, your father and I have been discussing expansion."

He wrapped his arm around Paige, drawing her into the shelter of his body. "You want to build another wing to the house?"

"No. Actually, we were thinking of enhancing the resort on Kauai and possibly acquiring some property on Maui. You wouldn't happen to know a good architect, would you?" She winked at Paige.

"Really?" The grin on Nathan's face was priceless. Crow's feet wrinkled the outer corners of his eyes, which sparkled with excitement.

"Really." Naomi's smile almost matched his.

He released Paige to gather his mother into his embrace and swung her around in a circle. While she softly laughed, he whispered, "I love you," against her ear.

"I love you too, son. Now put me down and let's get these pictures over with."

His mother was like a drill sergeant, lining individuals up next to Nathan and Paige for pictures, beginning with her, his dad and Cami. Next in line were Evelyn and Susan. His mother ordered a multitude of pictures be taken. As the big orange sun dipped into the water, the last of the arranged photographs were taken.

Everyone moved to the grassy area that hosted two large tents surrounded by tiki lights that glowed red and green with the Christmas theme. Inside the tents, elegant white tablecloths and votive candles flickered in the breeze. Hawaiian music played in the background, and then the song that she and Nathan had chosen five years ago to be played at their wedding began. Through the speakers George Jones' twangy voice sang, "Walk through this world with me. Go where I go."

Nathan held out his hand to Paige. "Will you walk through this world with me?"

A tear rolled down her cheek as she placed her hand in his. "For eternity."

He led her upon the makeshift dance floor and pulled her close to him. His cheek nestled against hers. He stepped forward and they began to dance. In his strong arms Paige waltzed through the clouds. Those looking on didn't exist as they drifted around and around the floor.

All too soon, the song was over. Yet they didn't release each other. He gazed deep into her eyes and whispered, "Let's cut the cake."

"I'm all for that."

Cutting the cake wasn't exactly next on Naomi's schedule. First there was the toast and dinner. As Nathan and Paige sat at the table of honor sipping champagne, his mother approached. "I had the beach house set up for your honeymoon suite. Janis and I will make sure Cami is preoccupied while the two of you slip away. That is, after you cut the cake."

Finally. Paige rose even quicker than Nathan did. They both received a daunting frown from Naomi.

In seconds they stood beside each other holding the knife above the beautiful cake. The blade sliced through the sweet confection. As each of them took a bite of the other's cake, the crowd cheered. They moved away from the table as others stepped forward to accept a slice. It was a perfect opportunity for them to escape.

Barefoot, they moved like two thieves in the night. When they were far enough away so that no one could hear, they burst into laughter. Hand in hand, they ran toward the small cottage set off from the rest of the mansion.

Nathan opened the door. She wasn't prepared for him to

scoop her up in his arms and carry her over the threshold, but it was a charming gesture. Snaking her arms around his neck, she held on tight.

The cottage was adorned with silky curtains and snowy white petals spread across the floor leading to the bedroom. The lights were dimmed. As he carried her through the room, she breathed in the beauty of the moonlit ocean licking the beach through the open picture window. Stars twinkled in the darkened sky. Softly burning candles were scattered around the room. The light scent of vanilla and cinnamon filled the air. It was everything she had ever dreamed of.

When her feet touched the ground, she turned in his arms and captured his mouth with hers. Desire hummed across her flesh. She slanted her head and deepened the kiss.

The whisper of her zipper falling sent a shiver down her back. She clung to him, not wanting the caress to end, but anxious to consummate their marriage. Even when her dress lay in a cloud of white at her ankles, she didn't release him.

"I need you naked." The ache in his voice made her breathless with need. Gently, he eased her arms from around him and began to peel one garment and then the next from her body. "So beautiful."

What she would give not to have been so battered and bruised for her wedding night, but even her condition could not cloud her joy.

He ran his palms up and down her arms. "I'm so sorry about the other night."

She reached for his shirt. "It's in the past." Only the future lay before them. With each button that loosened, her arousal skyrocketed. She wanted this man—her husband—inside her, loving her. Her nipples tightened, her breasts heavy with need. When she tugged at his belt, pulling it from each of the loops, moisture anointed her thighs. Before she could unfasten his pants, he took her into his embrace.

The feel of their naked chests, skin to skin, made her arms prickle. He trailed a path of wet, warm kisses along her neck and shoulder blade. *Yes.* She lolled her head back and savored his caress. He folded his arms around her, palms smoothing down her back to cup her ass, and pressed her firmly to his engorged erection.

Her inner muscles flexed, sending a shiver along her vaginal walls. "Now, Nathan. Love me."

Nathan laid her on the bed amongst the flower petals, and a tremor raced through him. This woman was his wife—his life. His hands shook as he reached to unfasten his pants. A tug at his zipper released the pressure against his cock, which grew even harder when she arched her body wantonly, an invitation to join her.

She was everything he'd ever wanted.

He crawled upon the bed and lay beside her. His palm lightly skimmed her black and blue rib cage. "I don't want to hurt you. Tell me what to do."

"Touch me," she whispered.

That he could do.

The tips of his fingers brushed against the satin of a breast, raising small bumps along her areola. Her nipple was so taut he couldn't help bending down to taste the salt of her skin. He tongued the tender skin, and the bead hardened even more. She smelled of jasmine and a beautiful future. With soft kisses he made his way up to her neck. A soft moan slid from her lips, vibrating against his mouth as he caressed her throat. He brought a hand up to pluck the naupaka flower from her hair and laid the blossom gently on the wicker nightstand.

Her palms smoothed up the muscles of his forearms and biceps, before she looped her arms around his neck. With a nudge she pulled him down to meet her lips. Her honey taste was seductive. When their tongues met, slid together, he swallowed her sigh.

She moved her leg so that it caressed the length of his erection. "I need you inside me."

Nathan started to ease atop her and then stilled. Would she panic beneath his weight, feel trapped? He rolled back to his side.

The skin of her belly was soft and warm as he caressed his hand downward. He ran his fingers through her pubic hairs, and then farther to feel her heat, her wetness. Swollen and slick, he pushed past her slit, burying a finger deep inside. Her hips thrust against his hand. Another finger slipped inside her. When his thumb applied pressure on her clit, she cried his name. Her thighs sprung wide.

"Baby, the way I see it is you can either straddle me or I enter you from behind."

"I don't care. I just need you." He loved the urgency in her voice. Her chest rose and fell rapidly. Her tongue slipped between her lips, savoring his taste. Damn. That was sexy. The pulse in his balls picked up the pace, and the flow of blood into them was fucking hot.

"Come here." He lay on his back. "I want to see your face when I take you for the first time as my wife."

She looked down at him with a tender smile that turned heated when she threw a leg over him. Straddling him, she pressed her slick heat against his cock and rocked back and forth.

"Damn, Mrs. Cross, that feels good." He smoothed his palms up her bruised rib cage to the curve of her breasts. Even

196

the delicate mounds hadn't made it through the mudslide untouched. Scrapes and cuts covered her velvety skin. Cupping her breasts in his hands, he cradled them, feeling their weight. His thumbs played across the hard tips.

"Mrs. Cross. Hmmm. I think I like the sound of that." She reared back and angled her hips so that when she lowered herself, his erection was at the center of her pussy. Achingly slow, she eased him into her warmth until he was seated deep inside.

They fit together perfectly. Her body molded around him, held him in a tight fist of sensation. When she began to move, it was pure heaven. His hips met hers in an easy rhythm, one meant for just the two of them.

Her eyelids fell halfway shut, a drop-dead sexy expression on her face that was nearly his undoing. Electricity tingled down his shaft. The tremble in her thighs and the quickening of her breaths revealed that her orgasm was close. He grasped her waist, driving her down hard. At the same time, he ground his hips. The sensitive slit on his erection burned with pleasure.

She groaned. Gasping, she rolled her hips forward, a slow stroke that built into a flame of pleasure, sending his blood pumping.

"Sonofabitch." His voice trembled. "I don't know how much longer I—" He wasn't prepared when a series of strong contractions squeezed him. His mind went black except for the starburst behind his eyelids. A strained cry tore from his throat as his control disintegrated in flames. Lord, help him. Her pussy was a furnace, sending arcs of lightning down his shaft to rip air from his lungs. He shook with the fervor, the love that poured out of him into his wife.

Paige couldn't move. Her body vibrated with the intensity of her climax. Every nerve ending felt alive, hot, as if sparks burst from each pore. Their moment together was poignant, but earth-shattering at the same time, everything she had expected when they consummated their love.

She opened her eyes to see Nathan staring at her. He wore a sated grin.

Had he felt what she had?

When her pussy stopped fluttering, she lowered herself upon his damp chest, and he wrapped his arms around her. She snuggled closer, allowing the cool breeze to chase the heat from her body.

"That was," he sighed, "unbelievable."

It tickled her that he had experienced the same mind-blowing orgasm as she had. In fact, this was the best she'd felt in the last five years. "Tell me all this is real. That I'm really your wife."

He rolled her onto her side and spooned her with his body. "You better believe it's real. I have the papers to prove you're mine, Mrs. Cross."

She couldn't help the girlish giggle that bubbled from her throat. "You have no idea how much I love you."

"Yes I do. Because I feel the same way."

They lay there for several minutes, unmoving and silent, while she listened to the ocean and wind outside.

"You okay?" he asked.

"I'm more than okay. I'm perfect."

He eased her to her back and stared deep into her eyes. "Merry Christmas, Paige."

"How could it not be merry? You've given me everything I could ever want—you."

His smile was priceless as he leaned over her and kissed her like a man in love.

Her one and only love—her husband.

About the Author

A taste of the erotic, a measure of daring and a hint of laughter describe Mackenzie McKade's novels. She sizzles the pages with scorching sex, fantasy and deep emotion that will touch you and keep you immersed until the end. Whether her stories are contemporaries, futuristics or fantasies, this Arizona native thrives on giving you the ultimate erotic adventure.

When not traveling through her vivid imagination, she's spending time with three beautiful daughters, three devilishly handsome grandsons, and the man of her dreams. She loves to write, enjoys reading, and can't wait 'til summer. Boating and jet skiing are top on her list of activities. Add to that laughter and if mischief is in order—Mackenzie's your gal!

To learn more about Mackenzie, please visit www.mackenziemckade.com. Send an email to Mackenzie at mackenzie@mackenziemckade.com or sign onto her Yahoo! group to join in the fun with other readers and authors as well as Mackenzie.

http://groups.yahoo.com/group/wicked_writers/

They say cowboys don't cry…
Apparently they don't forgive and forget either.

Second Chance Christmas
© *2007 Mackenzie McKate*
A story from The Perfect Gift

After four years, Lori Dayton is returning to Safford, Arizona to spend Christmas with her family and face her past. She has reservations about seeing Dean Wilcox again. But time hasn't changed her. She still loves Dean more than ever.

Time heals all things… Yeah right! Lori still heats Dean's blood like no other woman. Even after all she's done, he can't resist the urge to take her in his arms, feel her body pressed to his. He wants her naked against him, just like before.

Can he forgive her, as well as himself, for that dreadful night when they lost so much?

Warning, this title contains the following: explicit sex, graphic language.

Available now in ebook from Samhain Publishing.
Also available in the print anthology The Perfect Gift from Samhain Publishing.

Enjoy the following excerpt from Second Chance Christmas...

This was gonna be a helluva night.

Two large fans whirling above Lori Dayton did nothing to ease the sultry flush across her skin, or the increase of her pulse. One set of fiery blue eyes across the room was responsible for her sudden reaction and the instant tightening of her nipples. The man she'd dreamed of for the last four years moved determinedly from the entrance, straight across the dance floor, and past the wraparound bar, toward the poolroom situated at the far end of the establishment where she stood. He didn't speak to her nor did he approach. But he was close—too close.

Focus and forget about Dean Wilcox.

He had clearly forgotten about her.

She diverted her gaze from his hot glare, choosing instead to study the intricate pattern of the tinsel draping the limbs of the large Christmas tree stuck in the corner. It must have taken hours to separate and lay each silver strand precisely an inch apart.

In the distance, she heard the band begin to warm up and laughter rang. The scent of cigarettes mingled with a variety of perfumes and colognes. A beer bottle or glass crashed to the floor. The loud, brittle sound startled her, making her heart lodge midway in her throat. Normal barroom noises, so why was she nervous?

"C'mon, sis, call your shot," Mitch, her partner and brother, impatiently encouraged. His eyes were fixed on the table as he chalked his stick. Will and Lance Carter had challenged them to a game of pool. She hadn't wanted to play, but Mitch never turned down a challenge.

Two local gals had their hungry gazes pinned on Mitch's muscular six-three frame like it was hunting season, and he was their quarry. They sat at a high-top table across the way, but looked like they wanted to slink across the room and wrap themselves around him. All three of her brothers were babe material—they had golden hair and eyes to match.

Women thought her brothers were hot, but as far as Lori was concerned, no man came close to the raw sensuality Dean Wilcox oozed. When the two gals who had been eyeing Mitch now ogled Dean, Lori realized she wasn't the only one who thought so.

"Earth to Lori." Mitch pulled her from her thoughts.

Focus.

Narrowing her eyes, she sized up the table. Pool stick in one fist, she dragged the other hand along the cool railing, moving slowly in search of the best shot. She fought not to look at Dean, not wanting to let him know he affected her, but she couldn't help raising her eyes to meet his.

With a condemning stare, he watched her. Only six feet away, he stood with his legs were wedged apart, unyielding arms folded across his broad chest. His stance screamed that if she drew any closer to him he would still be miles away, still be untouchable.

Forget him.

"Eleven ball, corner pocket." It would be a stretch, but it appeared her best choice. Leaning forward, she lengthened her five-seven frame across the table. With a jerk of her head she tossed her long blonde hair over her shoulder, and then positioned her fingers—

Well fuck. Her eyes were focused on Dean's zipper, which was directly in line with the corner pocket. The impressive bulge revealed he was erect, hard. The muscles in her throat tightened as she swallowed. She knew that cock, knew its length and girth, the way it felt sliding between her thighs, filling her to—

Her heart began to pound. What's the matter with me? Lust—nothing more. Remember the man hates you.

To make the situation more uncomfortable, when she leaned farther down, her T-shirt gaped to give him a direct, unhindered view of her bare breasts—helluva time not to wear a bra.

Dean made no attempt to look away. Instead, his eyes darkened. His nostrils flared.

And just like that her concentration flew out the door. Adios! It was gone in a heartbeat.

Once again she found herself thinking of him. Her vaginal muscles clenched as she imagined his strong hands touching her breasts, stroking the ache inside her. Her panties dampened.

She licked her suddenly dry lips, blinked.

Focus.

It wasn't like he hadn't seen her breasts before. But each time she slipped the stick back and forth between the cradle of her thumb and forefinger, she thought of Dean buried deep and rocking inside her needy core.

Stop it.

With more force than she intended, she thrust her stick forward and struck the cue ball lower than anticipated.

In horror, she watched the spinning white ball raise from the felt, clear the rail, and nail Dean dead center of his groin.

They say cowboys don't cry...

Evidently, they do if hit squarely in the nuts. Then all bets are off. They crumble like a day-old cookie to their knees. At least that's what Dean did.

With a gut-wrenching "ugh", he folded over, cupping his jean-clad crotch. She caught a glimpse of his painful expression as his golden skin tone drained to a pasty white. Like a snowman in the middle of summer, he melted and dropped to his knees. His head followed, bowing low.

"Ouch," a choir of rowdy cowboys cried in unison, hugging their cocks. Then they began to laugh hysterically at their fallen friend.

Exactly what a man found funny about seeing another man getting his balls crushed Lori would never understand. Perhaps they were simply glad it was Dean and not one of them.

With a grin, Will retrieved the cue ball and positioned it behind the invisible boundary on the table. With ease, he stretched his tall frame over the ocean of green felt, then slid his pool stick through his fingers. "Mitch, your sister's been back, what—two hours? Already the men in Safford have to watch their gonads."

Lori restrained the urge to chuck the eight ball at his crotch. Instead, despite the warning in her head, she went to Dean's side.

Crouched down next to him, she inhaled the warm scent of Old Spice. A tremor visibly shook him. Her hand wavered awkwardly above his shoulder as she fought the need to touch him. "Anything I can do?"

He yanked his head up, tossing back locks of wavy, black hair from his face. Blue eyes watered with the effort it took for him to breathe. "Get away from me," he growled.

She flinched.

Those were the exact words he had spoken to her the last time she'd seen him. Funny they would be the first ones she heard returning home.

hot stuff

Discover Samhain!

THE HOTTEST NEW PUBLISHER ON THE PLANET

Romance, fantasy, mystery, thriller, mainstream and
more—Samhain has more selection, hotter authors, and
everything's available in both ebook and print.

Pick your favorite, sit back, and enjoy the ride!
Hot stuff indeed.

Samhain
Publishing
Ltd

WWW.SAMHAINPUBLISHING.COM

GREAT cheap FUN

Discover eBooks!

THE FASTEST WAY TO GET THE HOTTEST NAMES

Get your favorite authors on your favorite reader, long before they're out in print! Ebooks from Samhain go wherever you go, and work with whatever you carry—Palm, PDF, Mobi, and more.

Samhain Publishing LTD

WWW.SAMHAINPUBLISHING.COM

LaVergne, TN USA
04 November 2010
203533LV00003B/18/P

9 781605 048635